T0164832

I Hate Myself
and
Want to Die

Anna Young

Order this book online at **www.trafford.com**
or email orders@trafford.com

Most Trafford titles are also available at major online book retailers.

© Copyright 2011 Anna Grace Young.
All rights reserved. No part of this publication may be reproduced, stored in a retrieval
system, or transmitted, in any form or by any means, electronic, mechanical, photocopying,
recording, or otherwise, without the written prior permission of the author.

Printed in the United States of America.

ISBN: 978-1-4269-7229-4 (sc)
ISBN: 978-1-4269-7237-9 (e)

Trafford rev. 06/06/2011

www.trafford.com

North America & International
toll-free: 1 888 232 4444 (USA & Canada)
phone: 250 383 6864 ♦ fax: 812 355 4082

Part 1 Introduction

Chapter 1

In my mind, stabbing at my vein with a needle is a part of a normal life. It's what I've wanted since I learned that my idols were heroin addicts, back when I was in seventh grade. Since then, I strived to become a junkie. Living in Green Bay, Wisconsin, a relatively small city, finding heroin was difficult. Opiate pain pills, on the other hand, just fell into my lap. When I was nineteen, my father was prescribed Percocet, and a few months later they switched the prescription to Oxycontin. I soon began snorting the Oxycontin on a daily basis. This went on for a year and a half. I always had a supply, so I never had to go through withdrawal.

When I was twenty-one I moved to Appleton, Wisconsin, with my boyfriend at the time. This is where I met drug-dealing brothers. They sold Dilaudid 8 mgs pills and heroin. I had finally found heroin. The brothers showed me how to inject the heroin into my veins, at which time I became a daily IV drug user. The brothers were addicts themselves, and the heroin and Dilaudid would always run out before the end of the month. This is when I first got dope-sick. I was hooked. I began to doctor-shop when my drug dealers were out of drugs, always looking for Dilaudid. I'd sell the story of my being an AIDS patient with a CD4 count as low as thirty-one and a viral load of five thousand. I would complain of pain in my legs from a neuropathy. The jig worked most of the time. As a junkie I looked like death warmed over, and the doctors took pity on me and what they thought was my imminent death from AIDS.

After I spent a few months doctor-shopping, the doctors began to get suspicious. They stopped writing the prescriptions and made me for an addict; no doctor would write me a script. I would travel all around Wisconsin to go to doctors. One day I ended up visiting a doctor I used to go to when I was in high school. I gave him my spiel about AIDS and low CD4 counts with high viral loads. He wouldn't write me a prescription for Dilaudid, but he was going to write me one for Vicodin. He ended up leaving the prescription pad in the room alone with me. I tore off a page and wrote out my own script for Dilaudid.

After getting the prescription filled, I drove to Florida. I knew I was in trouble, and I stayed there for a month. I found a heroin connection there and decided to move down to Florida. I just had to drive back to Wisconsin to get my things. When I got back to Wisconsin, I got pulled over by the police and was arrested for prescription fraud. I was sent to jail straightaway. I was released the next day on a signature bond, and on advice of my lawyer I was in rehab the next morning, in a treatment facility to stay out of jail. I was looking at three years in prison for my crime.

Part 1

I've been on a binge, shooting and smoking cocaine for twenty-four hours straight. People have wandered in and out of my apartment all night; the stain of their presence is noticeable everywhere I look. My apartment lies in shambles. Everything I own is strewn on the living room floor. The TV drones on in the background. I can hear Elliot Smith's melancholy voice wafting on the airwaves from a CD-player on the floor.

The room is dimly lit by a few candles. Outside the sun is just peeking over the horizon on a beautiful spring morning. I can hear the streets full of cars buzzing by carrying citizens of this country on their way to work. Then there is me. High, pacing back and forth, watching as streetlights change from red to green to yellow and back to red from the windows in my living room and kitchen. I have no job.

My hair is in knots, and eyeliner is running down my face; I have blood smeared on my T-shirt and arms from the holes I have poked into my hands and arms with needles full of coke. I look like I recently committed a gruesome murder. I feel somewhat panicked, and I decide to look around my apartment for an Ambien. I hide them from myself. If I didn't, I would take them even though I don't need to. Ambien is a sleeping pill. I take them to bring me down from the cocaine. It keeps me from getting the trademark coke crash and helps me to get some sleep.

After searching for an hour, I finally give up looking for the Ambien. I turn my attention to an end table. There sits a baggie of white powdered cocaine and a box of baking soda. A few 1 cc syringes are scattered about. A spoon and lighter are sitting on the end table as if they are waiting for me. I pour a good amount of coke into the spoon, fill a syringe with some water, and push the water into the spoon with the coke. Using the cap of the syringe, I stir the mixture and drop my cotton in the spoon and suck the concoction into my syringe. I tie off my already-swollen hand with a shoelace, and my veins reveal themselves.

Before I start to mutilate my hand with this needle full of coke, I hesitate and think about what I am doing. I really hate this drug; all it does is make me anxious and nervous, and I am anxious and nervous naturally. What I really need is heroin, my drug of choice for the past two years; that is, until I got strung out, committed a felony, went to rehab, got kicked out of rehab, and found the local clinic that provides the methadone I am still on. So now I guess I am a methadone addict, and since methadone has a long half-life and my dose is high, it keeps me from getting high on heroin or any other opiates, such as Dilaudid. Here I am, and I need to get high off something. Coke is available, I have a connection, and I go on a binge.

It costs sixteen dollars a day for the methadone treatment, which I don't have right now. I spent it all on this binge; this waste of a binge. So I come to the conclusion that this one hit of coke won't hurt anything. In fact, it might help give me the push I need to figure out how to scrounge the sixteen bucks up. So I start stabbing at my hand until the blood finally blossoms into the syringe, and I push the coke home into my vein.

A burst of energy comes into me, and I feel like Wonder Woman. I try to enjoy the high, but it is fleeting. The first hit of coke is always the best. After that you're just chasing that high, and you can never get enough of the drug. I have been using too long. Now it's just a matter of trying to keep myself numb of all emotions.

On my couch lies a naked, sleeping man. He has been my partner in crime for the past twenty-four hours. His name is Corey. I met him while I was in rehab last winter. As I watch him slumber, he looks so peaceful, and I feel a sudden pang of jealousy rising in me. How can he sleep so peacefully while I am wide awake with the worst case of anxiety I have ever had?

I really need to go to the methadone clinic and get my dose, but I don't have the sixteen dollars it costs. I gave it all to Corey for this coke, and he spent it buying more coke.

Usually, when I am not on a binge, I go to the methadone clinic every morning and get my dose. The methadone really helps me. It keeps me from being so anxious all the fucking time, and

I don't feel like a strung-out junkie when I take my methadone regularly. I feel like a whole person again.

Most mornings when I get home from the methadone clinic, it's the best part of the day. I love being alone in my apartment in the morning, when it's just me and Eleanor, my little dog. I become so relaxed when the methadone kicks in, and Eleanor and I go for walks or watch morning TV.

This morning is not one of those mornings. This morning, all I want is the money to get my methadone and to get Corey's naked ass off my couch. Unfortunately I can't make him leave—he's the one who bought all this coke, and I owe him three hundred bucks. So I am stuck with a naked man on my couch sleeping off a coke binge.

Just then I remember the counterfeit fifty-dollar bill some guy gave me last night when I sold him some coke. At the time I was livid that I got ripped off, but now think maybe I can use it to rip someone else off. I grab the fake money out of my dresser drawer and put it in my purse. I am pleased with myself and my new idea.

Then I look over at Eleanor, my dog, and am filled with an overwhelming sense of guilt. How can I put her through this shit? She didn't get much sleep last night either, and now that the house has quieted down, she is finally getting a little shut-eye.

God, I hate myself. But when I really think about my life and the people in it, Elle is the only thing I truly care about. I have to stop this—if not for me, then for her—and I make a resolution to myself that this is it, no more dope. I know I can do it; I have done it before. I was clean for ninety days, until I fucked up.

Since I have the fake fifty, I decide that my best chance of cashing it is if I try to buy something with it and then use the real money I get back to pay for my methadone. I grab my keys and purse. Elle hears my keys jingle and runs into her bag that I use to carry her around. She has been carried in a bag since she was a little baby. I toss on a sweatshirt to cover my bloody T-shirt and try to make my face look a little less scary.

Elle is excited to be leaving and wags her little tail. I run out to where my car is parked, and before I get in, I let Elle out to go potty. The fresh air fills my lungs, and my resolve to stop using gets even stronger. When I am finished with all this shit I have to do to get my methadone, I am coming home and making Corey leave. I'll call the police if I have to. Then I am done; no more illegal activities for me.

Elle and I hop into the car and drive down the road a little ways to the gas station. I am already anxious from the coke, but knowing that I am going to try to pass fake money puts me way past anxious. I am about to have a heart attack as I walk in the door.

The cashier is a man in his fifties, with white hair pulled into a long ponytail in back. He looks like an old hippie. There is no one else in the store. It's too early for the usual transients who hang outside the front of this place. This is the store all the hoodlums loiter in front of, and that's the reason I picked this place.

I take a deep breath and ask for a pack of Basic Full Flavors. He grabs the smokes and rings them up. I hand him the money, and he quickly glances at it, turns it over, and then puts it into the cash register.

I just got away with a federal offense; I can't believe it. I turn around and leave. I am elated that I got away with it and now I can get my methadone. I jump in the car, put it in drive, and step on the gas, squealing my tires as I pull out. I want my methadone now!

As I am driving, my mind starts to wonder. Here I am high as a kite, I just committed a federal offense, and I'm on probation for the prescription fraud that I committed last year. The summer before I lost all conncetions for heroin and dilauded aka hydromorphone and getting sick, so I went to my doctor and asked him to write me a script for hydromorphone, a prescription narcotic, often called hospital heroin; he wouldn't. Just when I thought I was screwed, the doctor made the mistake of leaving me alone in the room with his prescription pad. So I ripped off one of the prescription papers and stuffed it in my purse. As soon as I was out of there I wrote out my own hydromorphone prescription and filled it at a Walgreens.

I got caught a few months later. I was unaware that they send all scripts back to the doctor's office for verification purposes; and he knew he never wrote me one for any opiates. Busted! That's how I ended up in rehab and met Corey.

After getting kicked out of rehab, I went to the methadone clinic. At the time I had to be in some sort of treatment to avoid jail. It worked, and I ended up on probation for a year instead of in jail for a year.

I pull into the methadone clinic parking lot, and Elle's barking like she always does in morning when we come here. She hates being left in the car, but I do it because it only takes a few minutes to dose; she's fine in the car alone for a minute or two.

I run into the clinic. Thankfully no one is in line today, and I go straight to the dosing window. Pat the nurse gives me a look like she knows that I am high. She hands me a little cup to pee in and says, "You have a urine analysis today."

I think to myself, *Fuck, I am totally screwed. My urine is definitely dirty with coke and God knows what else. Who knows what will happen when the results come back?* I go into the bathroom and quickly pee. While in the bathroom I'm shaking with anxiety. After I am finished I go back to the window and hand her my warm cup of urine.

"Here you go," I say as calmly as possible, trying not to let her see that I know I am screwed when the results come back positive for every drug known to man.

"After you dose, Kay would like to talk to you," she says as she fills my Dixie cup with the methadone.

"Okay," I say, taking the cup and slamming the methadone. At that moment I am just grateful to be ingesting the methadone. This means that soon my heart and mind will stop racing and I can rest.

I walk down the hall from the dosing window to Kay's office. Kay is my drug counselor at the methadone clinic; we usually meet once a month to assess how I am progressing. We already met this month, so I have a feeling this is not going to be a good meeting. I knock on her door.

"Come in. It's open."

I walk in and say, "Hi Kay, what's up?" I am still trying hard to hide my fear.

"Have a seat, Anna. We need to talk." She says this, and immediately I can tell I am fucked. "Do you remember calling me yesterday afternoon?"

Shit, I do remember. I called her with a needle in my arm, literally, and asked her for help: "Kay, I am using again, and I need to stop. I don't want to use anymore! Can you help me?"

She sort of brushed me off and told me to call someone from NA. I hung up and forgot about it, and now it has coming back to bite me in the ass.

"Well, Anna, I had to call your probation officer and tell him what you said. You do know that relapsing is grounds to revoke your probation."

I immediately started to sob. I had a feeling that something bad was going to happen, but I didn't predict anything this terrible. She grabs the phone, and seconds later she's on speaker phone with my PO.

"She's here. What do you want me to do?"

My probation office addresses me. "Anna, I am revoking your probation, for your own safety. There will be a police officer at the clinic soon."

Through sobs I tell him, "Elle is in the car, and I have no one to pick her up."

He pauses and thinks about what to do. Then he comes back. "Well, Anna, I will allow you to go home and find someone to take care of your dog, but you have to be at my office at 10:00 am. Don't even think of taking off. You will just make things worse."

I calm down a little after he says this. I tell him, "I will be there at 10:00 am sharp."

It is 7:30 am now; I have plenty of time to get things in order. Kay hangs up the phone and says, "I am sorry I had to do this. It's just that I am really worried about you. I hope this will keep you from hurting yourself any more."

I just walk out and don't even bother acknowledging her. I am so pissed; maybe I need help, but not punishment. So now I am going to have to withdrawal from 140 milligrams of methadone in jail. There is no worse place to go through opiate withdrawal than jail. That fucking bitch!

I jump into my car and speed away, hysterically crying. *I should have seen this coming*, I say to myself. I never get away with anything. This is God punishing me for passing fake money.

I look at Elle, and she looks so innocent. She has no idea what's happening, how bad things are. Maybe she does. She is licking my fingers like she is trying to make me feel better. I give her a kiss on top of her head as I pull into my parking space at home.

I get into my apartment and start making calls. First on the list is my ex-boyfriend Pete, Elle's daddy. I ask him if he can pick up Elle by 10:00 am, and I tell him why.

He says, "Sure, I'll be there around 9:45 am."

Next call is my dad, who lives four hours away in upper Michigan. I tell him the news, and he is upset. He thought I had been doing so well with the methadone treatment. He asks, "How long will you be in jail?"

"I don't know, Dad. Probably not too long. I didn't do anything that bad. I just relapsed. It happens to every addict at some point."

He says, "I will call your mom for you," and we say our good-byes.

Then I call my aunt Debbie, who has been helping me out since my mom moved to Hawaii a year ago for her traveling nurse job. Deb has been my surrogate mom since then, taking me to all my court dates and bringing me cigarettes in rehab; giving me money for the methadone when my mom forgets to Western Union me the money in time.

Deb is at work when I call, and her long-time boyfriend answers the phone. I give him the lowdown. He assures me that he will have her call me back in a minute. So I hang up and start to get ready for a shower while I wait for her to call back.

Two minutes later my phone buzzes, and sure enough it is Debbie, crying, worried about me. I try to calm her down and tell her I'm sorry.

"I haven't been using you all this time for money or anything like that. I just started using drugs again at the end of February, a month ago." I want her to know that not everything was a lie.

She's worried about Elle. Elle really likes Deb. Deb has no children, and she really loves dogs. I ask her if she would check up on Elle while she is with Pete. Pete lives with his dad behind a bar; Deb only lives about a mile away.

She says she would be happy to check in on Elle and make sure she is taken care of. She asks me to let her know what's going on when I know more and asks if I can use the phone in jail. I tell her I will, and we say our good-byes.

My last call is to my drug dealer. I need some Valium to help me through the withdrawals that are ahead. He answers, and I tell him the condensed version of events and ask him to bring me ten of his Valium. He says, "Sure, be there in ten minutes."

Corey is still lying on the couch naked, so I shake him and try to get him up and make him leave, but he is dead to the world and doesn't even acknowledge me. I give up and write a note and tape it to his chest.

Then I clean up the apartment and get rid of all drugs and paraphernalia. All the while I chain-smoke and stop to pet Elle every few minutes. I keep trying not to think about how much I will miss and worry about her.

Then there is a knock at the door. It is my dealer. He shows me the pills, and I give him the money I have left over from my previous crime that morning. Then he's gone. I'm sure he is off to his next sale. I take one Valium and head to the shower.

In the bathroom I look in the mirror and see how nasty I look. My skin is pale, with a grayish hue. My eyes have big black circles around them. The blue part of my eyes looks foggy, and the white part is blood shot. I am so disgusted I have to look away. I strip off the clothes that I have been wearing for a week. They are getting too big on me.

Since I started using coke, I have gone from my normal weight of 150 lbs to 130 lbs. It's really the only good thing about coke—the weight loss—but even that's not worth going to jail for.

I jump into the shower; the water feels good on my dirty body. I wet my hair and shampoo. I can feel all the snarls. My hair is really long, thick, and wavy, and I hate brushing it when there aren't any snarls. Now that it is a rat's nest, I don't want even want to get out of the shower much less brush my hair. I wash my body and condition my hair.

When I jump out Elle starts licking my toes as she always does. I grab my towels, wrap my hair, and dry off. Then I pull out my brush and start tearing out my hair, which takes fifteen minutes.

I glance at the clock: 8:30 am, tick tock, tick tock, tick tock, tick tock. Soon I will be in a cell, doubled over in pain from withdrawal. I am thankful that I got my dose today; this means I will have about forty-eight hours until I get really dope-sick.

Now that I am freshly showered, I put on some comfy clothes—a pair of black sweats and a clean white T-shirt. I sit down on the chair next to the couch and pull up the ottoman. I light myself another smoke and turn on the TV to watch the *Today* show.

I eat a few Hohos and let myself relax. Elle jumps up on my lap, and I cuddle her. I start to get sleepy, finally, now that my methadone and Valium have started to kick in. Every few minutes I have to pull myself out of a light sleep to check the clock.

The idea to leave and not turn myself in crosses my mind. If I did run I would go to my dad's house out of state, but I would have to drive my own car all the way up there, and my tags are expired. Plus I am sure that my PO will put out APB for me and my car.

With my luck, I would probably end up getting pulled over with Elle in my car, way out in the middle of nowhere, with no cell phone reception. Elle would have to go to some pound, and I would end up in jail. I could hide out somewhere until my dad drove down to get me, but where would I hide?

My PO is not stupid. He knows most places I would go. Then I still wouldn't have my methadone. There is no methadone clinic in upper Michigan. My dad has a prescription for 30 mgs of morphine, but he keeps it locked up in a safe when I am around. I figure if I just turn myself in, I should be able to get back on methadone sooner. I decide against running.

My phone rings. It's Pete. He is outside the apartment building and needs me to open the door. I run to let him in. First thing out of his mouth is 'Jesus Christ, Anna, can't you stay out of trouble for one year?"

I give a little laugh. "I know I fucked up again. Thank you so much for helping me out in a pinch."

He gives me a look of pity and says, "Eleanor is my dog too, so it is my obligation to take care of her when you fuck up and go to jail."

Eleanor runs up to Pete, excited to see him. I start to cry again, realizing that I have messed up my life good this time. Pete was such a caring boyfriend, and I was whoring around, getting high, and stealing his money. He even took me back after every one of my infidelities. Pete is the one who bought me Elle two years ago, after I begged and begged.

I start to pack up Elle's things while Pete cuddles her. He looks at Corey lying on the couch and rolls his eyes. I can tell he feels uncomfortable after he sees him. I look at the clock and tell Pete it's time to go.

Elle jumps into her bag, and all three of us head out to Pete's car. My PO's office is close to my apartment, so I light my last cigarette and take a deep breath. I am surprisingly calm considering my predicament, thanks to my methadone dose and the Valium I popped earlier.

Before I go to turn myself in I have to hide the nine Valium pills I bought. I wrap them in my cigarette cellophane and burn the top so the pills are sealed in; then I pull down my sweat pants.

Pete is astonished by my actions. "What the fuck! Well, I should not be too surprised—you are crazy," he says.

As I am shoving the little stash up my glorious vagina, I say matter-of-factly, "I am going to need these in there."

I pull up my sweats up, kiss Elle good-bye, look at Pete, and say, "I am sorry for everything. You deserve better," and I am off.

I hate being separated from Eleanor; leaving her literally breaks my heart. Going through withdrawals and worrying about my baby girl—this is going to be brutal.

Chapter 2

I walk into my probation officer's office, and before I can say a thing, I am turned around and handcuffed. Two uniform police officers escort me to the police car. I ask as politely as I can if I can have a smoke, but neither officer says a word.

They just push my head down and shove me into the back of the cruiser. When I am in the car, I ask, "Where are we off to, boys?" trying to be funny. I am surprised at the answer. "St. Mary's Hospital; you have to be cleared medically to go into jail."

When we arrive at the hospital, I have to walk into the emergency room, handcuffed and escorted by both officers.

I'm alone in the room; my escorts are waiting outside the door. My mind is racing as I wait for the doctor to see me. I have manipulated doctors before— how can I get this one to say I am unfit to be locked up in a jail?

As is my luck today, nothing is coming to me, not a single idea. Then the door swings open and a cute young doctor walks in. He has a look of disgust on his face. His face says, "You're not going to pull one over on me, junkie."

He takes my blood pressure, asks me a few questions, and says something along the lines of "It will only feel like you're dying."

"Withdrawals are painful, and the depression you will feel is going to last a long time, but you will be better off in the long run if you stay off drugs," he says.

I look at him pleading with my eyes and ask if he can write me out a script to a nonaddictive anti-anxiety med. He immediately says, "No way; you need to do this cold turkey."

I can tell that he is doing this because he has something personal against addicts. Perhaps he has a family member who screwed him over while on dope and now he is taking it out on me. Most doctors would write something nonaddictive, or at least they would give me a note allowing me to take Tylenol PM.

I have gone through withdrawal before, and the insomnia is the worst part; in jail this will be intensified tenfold.

The doctor leaves the room and says something to the two policemen, and then he is out of sight.

I am transported over to the jail and fingerprinted, my mug shot is taken, and I'm escorted to a changing room. A female guard is my new escort at the jail. She is short and thin, with short brown hair. She has an ugly underbite. She gives off the vibe of "bull dyke."

She hands me a pair of orange jump pants and an orange top. "Brown County Inmate" is written on the back of the orange shirt. She lets me wear my own white T-shirt that I wore in and hands me a pair of used white undies and a dingy white sports bra.

On the wall next to us there are three dressing rooms with flimsy curtains as a door. I step inside the little room and strip down. Then I get nervous about my stash. So I dig two fingers up into my vagina and pull out the package. The whole time I am trying to be as quiet as possible. The bull dyke is only five feet away.

When I finally get it out, I tear open the cellophane and eat all of the Valium. It tastes chalky as I chew, and it's hard to swallow, but I manage to get them all down. I dress in my new uniform and step out.

I'm lucky that I just ate those pills, because now I get my cavity search. The bull dyke tells me to pull my pants down, bend over, and cough. I do as I am told, and I have to take my mind to someplace else.

I think about the pills I just took and wonder if I will overdose. If I do and they catch me before I am dead, I could go to Brown County Mental Hospital to detox. That sounds like best-case scenario. Most likely I will just sleep for a day or two.

All these options are better than being caught with the Valium on or in me and catching another charge. After the cavity search I am escorted by the bull dyke to the cell block where all new inmates go.

As I walk into my new home I notice that all the cells are lined up on the back wall. The rest of the walls have two-way mirrors so the guards can see inmates at all times.

The rest of the room is an open space. All the walls are grey cement, and the room is brightly lit by florescent lights. In the open space is a round table with four round stainless-steel seats with no backs. This area is called the dayroom.

There are two other girls sitting in the dayroom. Both are watching soap operas, and I don't look too closely at them. I am too tired by now to do much of anything, much less talk to criminals.

I have been wide awake thirty some hours and just took 90 mgs of Valium on top of 140 mg of methadone. I walk straight to the cell the bull dyke pointed out as mine. I am carrying a gray wool blanket and a white sheet and a thin green mat, like they give kids at daycare.

I roll all this out on my bunk and get settled. There is not much to the eight-by-six cell. There is a metal framed bunk bed. I don't have a cell mate, so I take the bottom bunk. There is a little table with a little seat next to it; I assume it to be used for writing. The toilet and sink are stainless steel and are connected to each other. The toilet seat has no seat, just a rim, like when your boyfriend leaves the seat up and your ass falls in.

There are no bars on this cell block. The doors to each cell are made of a thick metal, and there is a window toward the top of each door. Next to the door there is an intercom, with a button you can push in an emergency. I make a mental note of this while I lie down and fall asleep.

The next thing I know, three days have passed. I have been in and out of consciousness for the past three days, from the Valium no doubt.

I hear my name over the intercom, alerting me to the fact that I need to gather my things and get ready to move to general population. My head pops up off the mattress. My hair is matted, and my clothes are soaking wet from sweat. My legs are cramped up in charley horses, and they keep kicking and moving by themselves.

My stomach is churning, and I can feel my bowels ready to blow out of my butt. It takes every ounce of my energy to gather up my belongings and walk out to the dayroom to wait for my escort to gen pop.

I hear the metal-on-metal noise of a key being placed in a lock and the click of the lock disengaging. A fat, tall, white man with a crew cut and mustache walks in and grabs my arm to bring me to my next home within this hellhole.

I am beginning to wish that I was dead. I already feel like a dead man walking the green mile. We walk down some long corridors, I keep having to stop and catch my breath every few feet. The corrections officer has to hold me up or my legs would give out. He is wearing plastic gloves, because he is afraid to touch my sweaty body. He says nothing but what the necessary directions are.

When we get to an open area I can see into a big dayroom. There is a girl braiding her hair in the two-way mirror. Then the guard pulls out his keys and inserts one into the lock. The door opens to a room twice as big as the first cell block I was on, but other than size and the number of cells on the back wall, this block looks identical to the last one.

The first thing I notice is that all the women are separated into races—blacks, Mexicans, Native American, and whites. There are twenty women on this block, two women to each cell. There is a tiny shower next to all the cells. A blue shower curtain is the only thing between you and the rest of the inmates.

I've shown up just in time for lunch. I am not at all hungry, but I take a tray. I have been in jail a few times before, but never for more than twenty-four hours. I know that food is like money in jail. It is against the rules to share food, but everyone does it.

I sit next to the five other white women. Two of them I assume are around my age, twenty to twenty-five. One is sort of good-looking, almost like she does not belong here. She is the one who asks me first for my food. I ask her who is holding any kind of opiates.

She says, "No one. Why? You sick? You sure look like shit."

I give her a look that says she is correct in her observation, not able to make words. I am just too weak to do anything. I sit at the table until she is finished eating only so I don't get caught giving her my food.

I walk into my new cell; it is lock down after lunch, so my cell mate is in there with me. She is a middle-aged Indian, a little overweight, with thin, long black hair. She gives me a sideways glance and mumbles, "Don't shit or puke on my things, and try to hold everything in until I am able to get out of this cell." I nod yes and lay my head down to ease my headache from the bright lights.

I just sit in my bed and shake, sweat, and groan. Once in a while I drift off to sleep. I dream about Elle and getting high, and then I am startled awake.

I stare at the ceiling looking for a spot to hang myself.

Lock down is done and I am alone again. I am now determined to kill myself. I go over what I am going to write to my mom and dad and Pete in my suicide note.

I have caused nothing but problems for everyone I love. My parents already lost a daughter, in a drunk-driving accident in July 2003. She was my only sister; we are thirteen months apart. She was only nineteen when she died. I still haven't healed from the loss, and neither have my parents. I know that if I die, my parent would end up killing themselves. I can't have their deaths on my conscience.

I decide that an attempt would be a better chance of getting out and going to a hospital to detox.

I remember that before I went into rehab last winter I went to detox at Brown County Mental Hospital, and there was this man who tried to hang himself in jail. He ended up getting out and coming to Brown County Mental Hospital.

I think maybe they'll do the same thing with me, so I start to make my plans. Ten o'clock rolls around, and we are locked down for the night. Now is the time to attempt my escape plan.

I use all my strength to jump out of bed. I have a pencil, the only sharp object I could find, in my hand. I start to scream at the top of my lungs, "I have to kill you, and then I have to kill myself." My cell mate looks confused and scared. She throws her arms over her face. I push the intercom and scream, "Voices are telling me to kill her and myself."

Suddenly I hear an unlocking noise and see two men bull-rushing me. Next thing I know, I am down on the floor, and I immediately go limp.

I am still crying uncontrollably when they carry me out of my cell. One of the corrections officers goes to call someone, and the other one sits with me. He starts to say, "You have two options now: you can willing strip down and go to solitary confinement or you can fight us and be put in five-point restraints."

I opt for naked solitary. At least I can be sick in peace and quiet. I am put in my new cell. It just has a cement bed and the same sink-toilet combo every other cell I've been in has had. I hand the man my clothes, and he hands me some kind of pad apparatus to cover myself with. It is blue and feels and looks like those bibs they cover you with when you get an X-ray.

Then he is gone and I am alone. A few minutes later a woman shows up at my cell door. She has a nurse smock on. She hands me four different pills and a Dixie cup. I swallow them all and open my mouth to show her I did not cheek them. I don't bother to ask what they are, and she walks off.

A half hour later I am sleeping, dreaming about heroin and Eleanor.

The next morning I am awakened at 5:30 am by a man in a corrections officer's uniform. He is young with glasses, sort of cute with an innocent look to him. As he approaches my cell, saying my last name, I stand up in all my glory. I'm naked and shivering, and my hair is soaked with sweat. The only thing I have to cover myself with I used as a blanket.

I could not figure out how a person is supposed to wear it. The CO is shocked by my nudity and averts his eyes, almost like he pities me. He is carrying a Dixie cup in one hand and pills in the other.

He says, "Time for your meds, Young," and hands me the cup and meds through the little slot he opened, which I assume is used mainly to serve food. His eyes still averted from my body, he motions for me to show him my open mouth so he can make sure I comply with the meds. Quickly he looks at my mouth and says, "Good, breakfast is in a half hour."

As he turns to leave I ask if I can get my clothing back. "No, you will not get those back for three days, after you prove to us you are no longer a danger to yourself."

I sit down on my makeshift bed, on the floor, with my smock as bedding, and sigh. I am still junk-sick, and my legs keep shaking, but I try to think positive—at least I am getting meds.

I know that they have some sort of sedative in there, probably Librium. It used to be called mother's little helper and is now used mainly to treat alcohol withdrawals; sometimes they use it for opiate withdrawal.

I have never admitted to my Valium use, so the nurse does not know that I am also withdrawing from benzodiazepines, the main ingredient in Librium and Valium. I know I have to keep this to myself and play dumb about my knowledge of prescription drugs or I run the risk of getting momma's littler helper taken away.

If I can just keep getting those little helpers, this stay won't be the hell it was before my fake suicide attempt. I wait for the pills to do their job and try to meditate.

The days go on, and my sickness dulls. The depression takes hold, and I am engulfed by a thick fog of sadness. I eventually get my clothes back and make sure I follow every rule to the T.

I wait every second for word from my asshole probation officer; he is the only one with say as to when I am released from this place. I write him notes pleading and begging for my release and promising I will never use again, if I can just get out. I was even willing to go through residential treatment again.

I hand the corrections officer my notes addressed to my PO and ask if there is any word. Each time I hear a no, I feel like I have been kicked in the guts.

They are keeping me maximum security since my little adventure, and I am happy with this because I have a cell all to myself and there are only two other women on this maximum cell block. I don't have to talk to anyone.

If I did I would explode. I have such pent-up anger about my situation, and every hour I am in here without a word from my PO, I become more and more desperate. I am in constant worry that the nurse will take away the meds she prescribed me, so I make sure to let the COs know how much pain I am in.

Finally, after a full week behind a concrete and metal cell door, I hear my name on the intercom, with the words probation officer mixed in. I swear I heard the "ahhh" of angels, and I breathe a sigh of relief.

Before a have a chance to make myself presentable, I am escorted to the visiting area. Then I see him and his skinny little face with a smug expression. I can't help but smile, even though I hate this man; I know he is my only way out.

Before he can say a word, I say the first thing that comes into my head: "I am able to have an orgasm again. I couldn't before while on the methadone treatment. I didn't even have to masturbate; I just had a spontaneous orgasm." He looks at me, horrified by this sudden inappropriate outburst. I can feel my face get warm and red with shame.

He composes himself and gets to the task at hand. "I heard about your stunt. I know you were trying to get put in the hospital. If you hadn't done that, I was going to only hold you for forty-eight hours, but in the wake of it, I am not sure you are safe to be released even now."

I try to hold back my tears; I don't want him to know how easily he can rattle me. He is waiting for me to beg, but I don't. "Whatever you think is best, officer."

I go with the idea that I should just give him the power. Maybe he will see that I am not defiant. "I am allowing them to take you off max security and be moved to the work-release jail downtown. You won't have work-release privileges, but you will have the chance to prove yourself to be stable enough for release."

I don't want to ask him how long, but I can't help myself. I want out now! "How long will I be in there?"

"That is up to you, Miss Young. If you behave, I will find a spot for you in a residential drug treatment facility, but your future is in your hands. I do have the choice to revoke your probation completely and you will spend seven months in jail."

This gets my attention. I say, "I will behave. You don't have do anything like that." He gathers his papers and stands. I stand too, and the escort comes in to retrieve me.

On our trip back to my cell the CO tells me to gather my belongings, I am leaving on the van this afternoon to transfer to downtown jail. I really don't want to go there.

I have overheard the women talking about that jail. They say it is really old and dirty. There are five to six women to a cell. All the guards are assholes. You have to wait two days for maxi pads. They just let you bleed all over everything. Some cells don't have cameras, so if there is a fight you have to pray that someone calls for help. None of this is my biggest worry. The bathrooms in the old jail are supposed to be ungodly disgusting. Shit is smeared on everything; some of the women do not wash their hands, so everyone is getting sick. I still have diarrhea from withdrawals, and there is no door on the bathroom, so these poor women are going to have to hear and smell my shit. Then they will probably blame the filth on me and make me clean it. I would much rather stay in max, with my private cell and toilet, but not for seven months. That fucking asshole probation office knows what he is doing to me. He is going to make this jail stay harder than it normally would be, because I was clever enough to try to get myself out of jail and into a proper detox hospital. If only I didn't pull that stupid stunt. Librium is not worth a longer stay in jail.

I begin to gather my belongings and say my quick good-byes to the other two women in max. Time in jail goes by extremely slow, and I waited for two hours to be escorted to the transport van. It seems more like twenty-four hours, especially when you are unable to sleep. I read as much as possible, but the books available here are romance novels, not at all my taste. I really wanted something funny and inspiring, I needed something inspiring, I was losing parts of myself with each hour that passed while locked in a jail cell and treated as though I was some kind of violent criminal. I am no hardened criminal—I wrote a prescription out to myself for my own personal use! I never harmed another living thing in my entire life. I never would harm another living thing ever; yet here I am.

Sure I relapsed and used illegal drugs and then called and asked for help to stop using those illegal drugs. Does that really warrant imprisonment in a jail cell? Perhaps imprisonment in a treatment facility, but jail? Every moment I let my mind dwell on my perceived injustice, I become more and more disgusted with life, all life. The thought that this is happening over and over in this country to millions and mainly because of politics is sickening. The fact that I am uninsured and no treatment center will take me because of this means that I am just dumped wherever the system can find a place for me. If we had universal health care and decriminalized drugs, the country would be so much better off. But I know that money is the root of all evil, including this problem, and I will never change this nor see this changed in my lifetime.

In my depressed mind suicide seems like the only solution. If I was dead I would no longer suffer with this addiction, I would no longer be considered a criminal, and I would no longer hurt my family—except for the initial shock of my death, of course. Having experienced that initial shock after finding out my sister died in a car accident four years earlier keeps me from acting on my fantasies. I could not do that to my parents. After they are dead, though, well, that is a different story.

Finally I am escorted to the transfer van. First I am shackled; a leather strap is placed around my waist with chains leading to handcuffs and leg shackles. It is hard to walk with this around me, so a women in a police uniform helps me along and gives me a boost into the van. The van itself is a brown Dodge van, with one window in the back facing the driver's compartment. The seats are thin wooden benches. The skinniest ass would not fit on this bench, so mine is not fitting at all, and I am as uncomfortable as they can possibly make me. I am sure they were designed with this intention. Two armed police officer are in the driver and passenger seats up front. I sit as close to the front of the van's window as I can get. I have not seen the outdoors for seven days. Being able to look outside a window is a pleasure one does not appreciate until it is taken away. Watching the sky makes a day go by much faster than being in an artificially lit room 24/7. This particular day the sky is gray and the sun is hiding, but it is the most brilliant gray day my eyes have ever witnessed.

As the van merges onto the highway and cars are speeding past, I think about how these people have no idea what kind of cargo this van is holding. Me, a person, with a family, friends, a pet, and a drug addiction. These people are just going on with their daily routine as if nothing is wrong. I am, for a moment, awed by reality. This world could give a shit about me. Dead or alive, very few people even care. Life will go on after I am dead. I always knew this on an intellectual level, but now I feel it with every fiber of my being. I take it all in and cherish every second I am out of the jail. Every smell is intoxicating, every sight beautiful. I never want this ride to end.

Then we pull into the garage of Green Bay's downtown jail and the door shuts. Once again I am cut off from the world. Quickly I close my eyes and try to find those images and feelings in my memory. They are there, but not as vivid as they were a second ago. The van's back door is opened, and I scoot down to the guard standing there to help me out.

I walk into the work-release jail and notice that it is old. Everything is made of cinder blocks painted white. The hallways are narrow and loud from the air being pumped in from vents on the ceiling. There are no windows, and the doors are steel painted white, just like everything else. There are no windows on the cell doors. Behind each door is a cell housing up to six people at a time.

I am escorted to the third floor of the jailhouse and showed to my new home. Before I am permitted to enter I have to put my hands up against the wall and spread my legs to be frisked. I am deemed clean, and my escort unlocks the cell door.

I notice the smell first: it is feces, body odor, stale air, and smelly pussy. There in one square, grey table in the middle of the room with four plastic grey chairs next to it, The right wall has three little cubbies that hold bunk beds. Each bed is separated by a cinder-block wall. The bunk beds are made of steel and are painted white. On the back wall is a stack of lockers. Each one has number, and it is where we are to store all personal items. On top of the lockers is a stack of magazines and games. At the front of the room is where the bathroom is located. There is no light in the bathroom, and all I can make out is a porcelain toilet and a porcelain sink to left; to my relief, it is clean. Directly across from the bathroom is a small shower. The curtain is white and too short for the shower stall; again it is the only thing separating you from the rest of the women. The wall across from the beds is blank except for a nineteen-inch TV hanging from the ceiling. That is the extent of the cell and is what I have to look at for the next unknown amount of days.

Four women sit around the table. Two are white, in their early twenties and visibly pregnant. One has straight brown hair and a darker skin tone; the other has brown curly hair, blue eyes, and is really skinny. One is black and in her early thirties with her hair in a bunch of small balls. The other is an older white female in her late forties; she has short hair, glasses, and a gap in her front teeth. They are silently watching me as I put my bed together.

When I finish with that I walk over to the table and say hello. The black lady speaks up and says, "Girl, you have to take a shower; you nasty." This is true. I haven't showered since I have been in jail. I once tried to, and when I turned on the water I found that it is either super cold or super hot. My body could not take that kind of assault at the time and decided I would rather be nasty. Since I was in my own personal cell, who cared? Now that I am in close quarters with others I do need to shower.

I walk the three steps over to the shower and hear all the ladies giggle and mumble to each other about me. My face turns beet red, and I try not to show my embarrassment. I turn on the shower, and since the curtain is too short, water starts to seep onto the floor. I notice a chair next to the shower on the wall and realize that I need to put the back of the chair up against the curtain to keep this from happening. I can tell that the ladies are impressed by my ingenuity. I proceed to undress. Suddenly the black lady speaks up: "Hey, we don't want to see all your nasty shit hanging out all over. Get into the shower stall and undress." I jump into the shower stall, humiliated. The water is scalding hot, but I step into it and wet my hair and wash it with the soap packet given to me upon my arrival. This soap is bad for my hair, and I know I will never get the little black comb that was supplied through the tangles. I rinse out my hair and wash the rest of my body, and then I am done. I know I can't just jump out naked, and the towel you get in jail is a hand towel that doesn't cover anything; it doesn't even dry you completely. I do my best and reach for my clothes without showing anything the ladies deemed nasty. I put them on in the shower stall and step out. By now the girls are not interested in me; their shows are on. So I find my little plastic comb and begin the daunting task of combing my hair.

By now it is getting late, I go through the book bin and find a book, *Everything I Need to Know I Learned in Kindergarten*. This looks inspirational, and I settle into my hard bed with no pillow and read. After the guards turn off the TV the ladies turn their attention to me the new girl. The start tossing questions at me: What did you do? Where are you from? How old? Any kids? Did you really do the crime? How long you got? I answer each question politely and honestly, I can tell they are forming their opinions of me. I hope it's better than their first impression.

One by one they fall asleep, and I try to but keep waking up every half hour in a panic. Every dream is of getting high and Elle getting hurt. I go through the day's events in my head, analyzing and trying to figure out how I can work this to my advantage. I find no advantages and bring my mind back to the ride I got earlier in the day. Finally I fall asleep for the night.

The next morning I am awakened at 4:30 am for breakfast call and meds. This is a different routine than I was used to in the last jail. There I got up at 6:30 am for breakfast. All the ladies trudge out of their warm hard beds, rubbing their eyes from the sandman. I myself feel as though I had just fallen into a peaceful sleep a minute ago and am in a pissy mood from being roused so early.

We are served barely cooked blueberry muffins with fingerprints on them, an orange, a container of milk, and dry cereal. I only eat the dry cereal. After everyone is finished they go to the bathroom and then back to the beds. No one in my cell block is on work release, so we have nothing to do but sleep. The TV and phone are not turned on until 7 am. While everyone else falls back to sleep, I make my plan for the day. I will figure out how to use the jail phone and ask for the book bin and pick out three or four books to read. I drift off to an agitated sleep and don't wake until noon.

By the time I do wake my cell mates are engrossed in a soap opera. I ask the older lady to show me how to use the phone, which she does after some begging. I make my first call to my dad, and he is happy to hear from me. He asks, "How is it going in there?"

"Well, Dad, it is pretty shitty, I went through some horrible opiate withdrawals for the past week and ended up in solitary confinement until yesterday. That's why I haven't called."

"Are you feeling any better today?"

"They are giving me some Librium, and I feel okay for a few hours after I take one. But as soon as it wears off I am sick again. I just really want to get the hell out of here, Dad. Would you call my probation officer and try to talk some sense into him, make him see that I am a human being with a family who cares that I am suffering?"

"Sure, Anna, I will give him a call as soon as we hang up. I've got a lot of questions for him anyway. I will need his number, though; do you have it on you by any chance?"

Luckily I have it memorized by heart, and I tell him the number and we say our good-byes. I start to cry as soon as I hang up. I don't want him to hear me cry and make him more worried than he already is, so I hold in my sobs, and now I am a mess. The ladies look at me, annoyed. All they care about is that damn soap opera. They probably see this kind of thing all the time, with every new inmate who makes their first call to a family member. They themselves may have been in the situation at one time.

I go to my bed and just lie there listening to the TV and to the ladies talk about their lives and what they will do when they get out. The two pregnant ladies will have their babies in here and not be able to be with them after they give birth until they are released, six months after the baby is born. I feel so bad for them. I feel like such a sissy. Here I am crying about being dope-sick and lonesome, and these girls will not be able to bond with their newborns. I could have it a lot worse. I pull it together and focus on positives. I start to read a new book by the guy from *Everybody Loves Raymond*. It is a funny book and makes me feel much better.

Life goes on like this for five more days. I read and read and begin to socialize with my cell mates. They don't really like me, though. I am not sure why. Maybe because I keep to myself a lot. I start to sleep a little better, and this makes the days go by a little faster. Then I hear the key in the lock and the door opens. I am expecting it to be just another hourly guard check, but this time the guard calls out my last name.

I jump up and run over to her; my curiosity is boiling out of me. She says, "Young, your probation officer is here to bring to your drug-treatment program. Pack up your belongings and let's go—you're sprung."

Holy shit, I shout with joy. I can't stop smiling as I pack my things, and my face hurts. I am packed in twenty seconds flat and looking at the guard like a lost puppy dog eager to see its owner. She leads my down the long hallway to a stairwell where another guard is waiting for me and leads me to my destination.

I see my probation officer waiting for me, and when I see him my smile gets even bigger. Even though I hate this man with all my being, I can't let that outweigh the absolute joy I am feeling. As I am handed my street clothes and shown to the dressing room where I am to change, I feel like a kid on Christmas morning, receiving my freedom from Santa probation officer. I change slowly, enjoying this experience. It has been a long time since

I have this much happiness, and I want it to last. I slide on the black pair of sweat pants I wore into jail thirteen long days ago—the longest thirteen days of my twenty-four years.

My probation officer hand me some papers to sign on my way out of the jail. Then I walk outside into the brisk air, the ground is wet. It must have rained earlier in the day. It smells so fresh outside. I can smell the ground thawing after the long winter, and it is an earthy smell. The sun is covered by gray storm clouds, and the sky looks threatening, as if a lightning bolt is about to strike at any moment. My feet are in my own shoes, and the feeling is unfamiliar as I walk to the car my PO has motioned to as his.

I sit in the back seat, and he drives off. I can't help but look out the back window and watch the jailhouse get smaller as we drive away.

Chapter 3

My PO says, "You will be going to the Jackie Nitschke treatment center for drug and alcohol addiction."

I tell him, "That is where I went last time, when I was going to court and my lawyer advised me to volunteer myself into drug treatment. You know I was kicked out the week before I was to graduate, for using Benardryl to help me sleep. That was less than six months ago, right before Christmas. That's how I ended up at the methadone clinic. I can't believe they are going to take me back so soon."

"It took some doing, but you got a bed pretty fast. You'd better take this chance seriously, Anna. If you mess up this time, you will go back to jail, and this time for the full seven months you have left on your sentence. You will not be allowed to go back to the methadone clinic while you are under my supervision, so don't even think about that option, because it is not an option."

That pisses me off, but I don't say anything. I am worried that he will turn this car around and bring me back to jail. Methadone is drug treatment. Who the hell is this asshole to tell what kind of treatment I can or cannot receive? Oh yeah, he is my probation officer—my alpha and omega until my probation is up, in seven months.

I sit in the back seat, looking out the window and watching people as they walk to their destinations as I'm being driven to drug treatment by a probation officer. Right now I am so glad to be out of jail that rehab seems like it will be a vacation. I've been through it once, and I know the ins and outs. I should breeze though it this time. I have a lot more to lose this time if I end up getting kicked out again. I say a silent prayer to whatever might be out there. *Please help me get through this without going back to jail. I will do whatever it takes; just give me the strength to not use.*

The car turns the corner, and I can see the house. It is an old Victorian house, four stories including the basement. It is right smack-dab in the middle of downtown Green Bay. Next door to the treatment center is a crack house; across the street is the Village Inn, a fleabag motel where I used to go when I was homeless and came across enough money for a room and some dope.

As we pull in the parking lot, I look around for any sign of the others, but I look at the clock on the dash and it is 11:00 am, which means that all the other dope-fiend clientele is in morning group therapy. I unbuckle my seatbelt and step out of the car. My PO is right behind me as we walk up to the front door and I walk in. I go straight across the living room area to the office and see Rose, the same office attendant who was here last time I was here. I tell her I am here and that my PO is with me. She hands me a bunch of paper work and a pen.

"You know what to do—just go into the sunroom and have a seat. Watch the orientation video in the VCR and fill out your paper work." I look over at my PO and wave good-bye.

He says, "Remember what I said, and I will back once a week to check up on you."

"Whatever. Guess I'll see you soon." He turns and walks out. I go into the sunroom and get to the task at hand. I skim through the video and read the rules and regulations to make sure there have been no changes since the last time I read it. There haven't been any changes, so I sign my name to the papers and then just sit for a while to make it seem like I watched the whole video.

I decide while I am sitting there doing nothing that I will look through me purse and grab my smokes to get ready for a cigarette break. I notice that my cigarettes are not in there, and neither is my wallet or my cell phone. The jail must have forgotten them, or they lost them when I was transferred from maximum security jail to work release. I am mad, but not too mad. I don't need any of those things right now anyway. Well, the smokes I need, but I can call Pete or Aunt Debbie to bring me some. I have to call Debbie to bring my clothes and the rest of my shit anyway.

Enough time passes and I bring the papers to Rose, and I ask her if I can have one of her cigarettes. She says, "Sure." I tell her it will be my first smoke in thirteen days.

She says, "You should quit then. If you've gone thirteen days you don't need to smoke."

"Yes, I do, I have been under a lot of stress, and if I can't use dope I am definitely going to need to smoke. One thing at a time," I tell her.

"You're right. If I was in your position I would need a smoke too."

I make our way to the back of the house, where the smoke shack is, along with the picnic table and basketball hoop. The smoke shack is where everyone gathers in between groups. It is not often you get to enjoy a smoke by your lonesome here. I take this rare opportunity to pick my nose. I have not been alone in long time; I can eat my boogers if I want to, and so I do.

Rose gives me five minutes, and then she comes and gets me. She says, "I have to give you a tour. It will be quick since you know your way around already."

We walk up the steps to the second floor, which is the women's floor. There are five bedrooms with two beds to a room, and there is a group therapy room. At the end of the hallway is a bathroom with a stand-up shower and a porcelain toilet and a mirror over the sink. I think to myself, *Thank God. I can take a nice lukewarm shower and dry off with a nice big fluffy towel in private.*

Rose shows me to my room, and it's the same room and bed I had last time. I lie down on the bed and take in how soft a mattress feels and how good it feels to have a pillow and soft blankets. All these luxuries I had taken for granted my entire life. Not anymore. I am going to cherish the little things from now on.

We move on to the rest of the house. The third floor is the men's floor, with five rooms and one group therapy room. They also have a bathroom, but there is no shower in it. The men have to go to the basement or the first-floor bathroom to shower. We make our way back down to the first floor, where the kitchen and dining room are. Rose asks if I am hungry. "Oh yes, I am very hungry. I haven't had anything good to eat in thirteen days." I make myself a peanut butter sandwich with a banana and glass of Kool-Aid.

Every bite is like heaven. I scarf it down as if I will never eat again. To have moist bread and Jiffy peanut butter is like a religious experience.

Rose tells me to hurry. She wants to me to get to group before it's done so I can introduce myself to the other clients before we have to eat lunch together. I clean up the mess I made in the kitchen and make my way to the second-floor group room.

I walk into the room, and everyone looks up at me. Pam, the counselor, says, "Hi there, Anna. I was expecting you. We are just finishing up, and then we will do introductions."

I know Pam very well, from last time. She is the youngest counselor on the staff, but she never told me how old she was. I would guess she is in her late twenties or early thirties, She is five foot ten, with long legs. I guess she goes about 180 lbs, and she is fit. She has very pale skin, which gets a red rash when she is annoyed. Her breasts are huge. She is always dressed very nicely, in tight-fitting sweaters and expensive jeans. Her hair is straight, long, and blonde, always perfectly done.

She is soft-spoken and looks directly at you when speaking to you. I hate that. I have a hard time making eye contact when speaking to anyone. She was my "one-on-one" counselor the last time I was here. At first I really liked her, but then I realized that she was not an addict herself and had absolutely no idea what I was going through. Sure, she's seen a lot of addicts and went to school and learned about addicts, but in reality she has no idea. She also has a knack for spotting a lie, and last time I was here I was always lying. I learned to hate her.

As the group is finishing up I look around the room at my fellow drug fiends. The first person I notice is Jesse, a "long hair" with tattoos and a bad attitude; my sex drive comes flying back and hits me hard when I see him. I can tell he is fellow IV drug user, just my type. He has a hard body, and he is tall, his hair is blonde, and his eyes are blue. He wears holey jeans and metal band T-shirts. He notices me too.

There is one girl my age. She is skinny and attractive. Later I find out that her name is Erin and she is my roommate. Then there is another women, Alley. She is older, probably in her forties. She has thin stringy mouse-brown hair. She is super skinny and short, and she is the one who talks the most. That's it for women.

Then, including Jesse, there are five men. They are all quite a bit older than I am; one is black and the rest are white. They are all ugly and I assume are white trash alcoholics who smoke a little crack on the side. Jesse, of course, is the only exception.

As everyone goes around and introduces themselves, I find out that my assumptions are pretty accurate. Jesse and Ally and I are the only IV drug users in the bunch. I am the only opiate addict, and Jesse and Ally shoot coke. When they are done, I introduce myself and tell my story. As I speak, I am slouched in my chair, my eyes focused on my shoes, and I say everything nonchalantly. I want to give off the vibe that I don't care and that nothing will get to me. After I finish speaking, group is finished and we have a fifteen-minute break until we have to go on our walk before lunch.

I take off and go straight to the phone and call Debbie. I ask her to bring me ciggs and my clothes. I really want my shampoo and conditioner, my deodorant, my toothbrush, and most importantly, my makeup. I want to look and smell pretty for Jesse.

I call my dad too and let him know that I am out of jail and safe in rehab. He is relieved, but he says that he can still hear sadness in my voice and that he is worried. He says, "You're not going to anything stupid and try to kill yourself, are you?"

"No, Dad. I am not going to kill myself in here. Maybe if I have to go back to jail, but I promise I won't, Dad."

I hang up and go out to the smoke shack and bum a smoke from Ally, the only nonmenthol in the bunch. Everyone starts asking me questions; I answer them, even though I don't feel like talking. I remember how I felt when I was here last time. When someone new came in, that was the only excitement you had. It gets pretty boring hearing people's sob stories over and over, so when a new one comes in, you get to hear a new sob story, and you hope it is interesting.

Everyone is surprised to hear that I was a client here only six months ago. Jesse says, "So you're a hopeless case, huh." I just look at him, and give him a little smile as I take a drag off my cigarette.

After our walk and lunch, I go up to my room and find my roommate, Erin, on the phone. I pretend not to listen, but I am, and she is on the phone with a pharmacy ordering her Valium. When she is done, she looks over at me and says, "I know we are not supposed to have Valium in here, but I am crawling out of my skin, and I need it. It is not even my addiction. I am an alcoholic. You're not going to tell on me, are you?"

"No, I wouldn't tell on you, but when you get them will you give me some? I really could use some, but if you don't I still wouldn't tell on you."

"Sure I will give you some. If you take them too, then I know you are not going to tell on me."

I tell her, "You can't tell anyone else in here, not even someone you think you're close to. I have seen people get kicked out after telling someone they thought they could trust. It happened to me, with fucking Benadryl. I said something about it quietly to my good friend last time I was here, and somehow it got back to the counselors, and the next day I was kicked out."

She nods yes and says, "My lips are sealed; we won't even talk about it ever again. When I get them tomorrow, I will bring them up to our room and put them in your top dresser drawer. How many do you want?"

"Oh, how many are you going to get in your prescription?"

"I get sixty 5 milligram pills a month, and I only take one a day so I only use thirty pills a month."

"Well, I'll take as many as you are willing to give. Is twenty okay?"

"Sure, I will give you twenty pills, and let's not talk about it anymore."

I agree. The last thing I need is to get caught taking pills. Luckily she is getting Valium, because in jail I was given Librium, which is a benzodiazepine, so when I get a piss test here and I pop positive for benzos I can blame it on the jail meds. Benzos stay in your system for up to a month when you use them on a daily basis, and even before I was in jail, I was using them on a daily basis. It's like it was meant to be. I guess my prayer didn't work; I have no willpower.

The rest of the day is a bunch of group therapy sessions; same story, different person. They all go something like this: "I grew up a outcast, I have low self-esteem, and I started drinking in middle school. As I got older I started drinking heavier." Or if they are a drug user: "I started smoking pot in middle school as well as drinking. Then in high school I was doing acid and then snorting coke and then smoking it. At first it was no big deal, but suddenly it took over my life, and I was stealing and hurting everyone I love." Blah blah blah. Some were molested; some weren't. Some want to stop using; some are like me, forced into rehab by the courts or a PO.

At the end of the day, I find out that my "one-on-one" counselor this time is Ann. I know her from last time too. I like her. She is older, and she is from my hometown of Oconto Falls. She had heard about my sister's death and was sympathetic to me. She also noticed that I have mental health problems. I had been diagnosed manic depressive once during one of my stays in a nut house. I was prescribed meds for it, but I never got them filled after I got out. I just went on with life with my moods fluctuating and me using opiates to keep somewhat level. In my mind I am not so sure I am a manic; it seems to me that doctors want to put a label on everyone and everything.

Ann seems like she will be easier to manipulate than Pam was last time. I have to give her my drug history, starting with the first drug I used, including booze and beer, along with how much and how long I used them for. I do this, and it bores me to death. I did this last time I was here. The only thing new is my cocaine use. When I am done telling her my drug history, she says, "Well, Anna, you are in the right place. Your drug use has escalated, and I am worried that if you didn't find your way here, you would be dead."

I think she is being dramatic. In my mind the only thing rehab did for the me last time was to take the fun out of getting high. It was like after I got out of rehab. I was now a real drug addict, and that made getting high seem wrong. I don't dare tell Ann this. She would say something to my PO about it and probably think I don't want to be there. Which I don't, but I don't want her to know that.

In any case I am glad to be out of jail. When bedtime rolls around, I get ready for a nice, warm, private shower. Debbie brought my belongings earlier in the day when I was in with Ann. She got me Camel cigarettes. I smoke Basic Full Flavors, but the Camels must have been on sale. Debbie is very frugal, and I really don't care what kind of cigarettes I have as long as I have cigarettes.

I take a nice shower and put conditioner in my hair for the first time in thirteen days. Finally, I will not have to spend two hours combing through my hair, and it won't be frizzy when it dries. Debbie brought me a bunch of crime novels. Not my favorite, but better than romance novels or the *Big Blue Book* of Alcoholics Anonymous. I lie down on my nice soft bed, put my head on the pillow, cover up with the soft blankets, and read for a while. After my eyes get too tired to read I look out the window next to my bed. I watch all the cars driving by and wonder where the hell these people are going. I fall asleep, comfortable for the first time since this ordeal started.

The next morning I'm rudely awakened by my roommate. She alerts me to the fact that I have overslept. We are supposed to be out of bed by 7:00 am, and it is 7:30 am. We have to be in meditation by 8:15 am sharp. I sit up and look around, trying to get my bearings. I feel a wave of relief when I realize that I am in a soft bed and I can go outside when I want to and get a drink when I am thirsty. I can take a shit in private and spray air freshener if it stinks. This is the life, and it only gets better the more aware I become. Today is the day my roommate will be getting Valium; soon I will be nice and relaxed.

I brush my teeth and put on my makeup, with my usual black eyeliner around my eyes and dark brown eye shadow around my eyes too. I want to make sure I look like a junkie who doesn't care what people think, even though I do care, especially about what Jesse thinks. My eyes are what most people say are my best feature, and if I do say so myself, I have beautiful, very bright blue eyes. If you stare into them you can see my soul. The rest of my face is not so bad. I know I am not ugly, but I am no model either.

I put on a pair of worn-in jeans and a tight blue T-shirt that says "Crack is whack." It has a picture of a vial with two rocks of crack in it and a line through them, like on a no-smoking sign, on the front. On the back of the shirt there is a picture of a crack pipe and the words "Don't believe the pipe." Perfect for the situation, in my opinion.

According to dress code, shirts that are antidrug are okay to wear.

When I go down to the smoke shack, everyone reads my shirt. They all ask where I got it. I tell them I found it at a thrift shop a couple of years ago, which is a lie. I bought it for twenty bucks at a store in the mall. I am such a lame ass. I want to not care, but I care too much about not caring.

When I was high, I didn't care. Now that I am not on drugs, I care.

I sit down and light up a cigarette. Jesse is outside smoking along with all of the dope fiends. I listen to everyone. Lamar and James are talking about how good it feels to be clean and what they plan on doing once they get of treatment. Ally, the older lady, is talking to Erin about getting high; she talks and talks. No one can get a word in edgewise. I can tell that Erin is not listening too closely.

I keep quiet and think how much I fucking hate people. How I would rather put a pistol in mouth and pull the trigger than become like these people.

There is fifteen minutes until we have to go up to the group room for our morning meditation. I remember the daily schedule clearly. First up is half-hour meditation, where we sit in a group, listen to birds chirp from a stereo, and are not allowed to talk or read. Then we are off to three hours of issues group, which is hell. In this group we start out by "care fronting." This is where if anyone notices anything about another group member, be it good or bad, we are to confront them with it, but in a caring manner. For example: "Anna, I have noticed that you are glorifying your drug use."

Then the counselor says, "How does that make you feel, Anna?"

I would say, "It is really hard for me to be in rehab and not talk about my drug use. And when I talk about my drug use it is usually in a positive way, because I really loved getting high. Of course I know this is wrong. Would anyone give me some advice on how to change my perception of my drug use?"

Then someone in the group would offer me some lame suggestions, and the counselor would say something like, "Wow, I think we made some good progress here. Does anyone else have a care front or issue they want to bring up here in group?"

This goes on for three hours, and by the end I am frustrated and bored. I want Jesse to notice me, so before we start our next activity, I go up to him and say very blunt, "I want to have sex with you."

He looks at me, smiles, and says, "It'll cost ya a buck fifty."

"I can't afford that."

"You're out of luck then, little missy." Then his face get serious, and he says, "Why are putting on such a front? You we can see right through your 'I don't care' attitude."

I can feel my face flush with embarrassment. I wanted to impress him so badly that I took it too far and am no longer being myself. Without the comfort of opiates or methadone, I have no idea who I am or how I act. Nothing comes natural anymore.

I don't know what to say to him in defense of my attitude, so I don't say anything and go up to my room and wait for our next activity.

The next time slot is a fifteen-minute walk, followed by a half-hour lunch. During this time, all I can think is *when will she be getting that Valium?* As soon as we are finished with lunch it is off to another hour-long group and then another, and then we have our afternoon half-hour meditation. After meditation we are done with groups for the day.

Then we walk to an AA meeting at around 5:00 or 6:00 pm. AA is my favorite part of rehab. You get out of the treatment house, and you get to meet new people. Every day we go to a different AA or NA meeting. Now that I have my sex drive back, I scout out all the men at the meetings; none are as hot as Jesse.

I know that I am not ready to be in any kind of relationship. This is how I always get when I am not using dope—I get boy crazy. I fall in love with some guy and think about him all the time. Really, I become obsessed and scare the guy off. My heart gets broken, and I move on to the next guy.

This is one of the main reasons I started using dope. I am content to be alone when I am using. I don't need to be in love or obsessed with a guy. Fuck, I hate being in love. I don't know why I even do it. It's like I can't help myself. I hate myself and want to die.

During the whole meeting, I didn't listen to a word; all I could think about is getting some Valium in my blood. I try to make it look like I am listening because I don't want to get "care fronted" tomorrow in issues group.

When we get back from AA, we have free time, and we can watch TV downstairs in the living room area or play games in the dining room. We can also work in the basement on assignments that we were given in one of our groups. Mostly people use the phone and go out to the smoke shack and socialize with each other while smoking and drinking mass amounts of coffee.

I smoke a few cigarettes with Erin and then go up to my room. I open my drawer and find twenty little orange pills wrapped in cellophane. Erin came through. I take two of the Valium, and then I go find some masking tape and tape the pills under my mattress.

Erin is still down in the smoke shack talking on the phone with her boyfriend; she talks to him for hours. I will have the room to myself until ten, when we all have to be in our rooms. Eleven thirty is lights out.

I take a shower, put on pajamas, and hop into bed to write in my journal and read and wait for the Valium to take effect. We have to hand in our journals so the staff can read them. It is so nice to be alone in a room, lying on comfortable bed, able to eat or smoke whenever the urge hits.

Yet I cannot shake this fear I feel. I am terrified that I will screw up and be sent back to jail. What if the counselors don't believe me when I pop positive for benzos, which it is because of the meds they gave me in jail. I told Ann, when I first got here, to call the jail and get my records. I let her know that I would still be positive for benzos right away, even before I knew Erin would be giving me some.

What I really want is to get back on methadone treatment. I learned my lesson in jail. I won't be using illegal drugs anytime soon if I can just get back on methadone.

Well, yeah, I am using drugs in rehab, but I need those. I swear to God if I didn't have anything I would kill myself. I know I am an addict. The first step is admitting you have a problem and that you're powerless. I have that step down.

Do I want to stop using though? Yes and no. I want to stop using illegal drugs and stop sticking needles in my veins, but I still want to stay on the prescribed methadone. When I am on methadone, I don't need Valium. I don't need anything but methadone.

When I was on methadone, I stayed off all other drugs for ninety days. That is a fucking miracle. I hadn't been off drugs for more than three days in the past two years until I got on methadone.

Then I met Corey. I think it's because of rehab that I relapsed. If I had never met anyone in rehab last time and watched them all relapse, then I would not have relapsed. Everyone I was close to from this place on my last stay was only clean for at most two months after they left. Then when they relapsed, I had new drug connections that I did not have before. This place made it easier for me to get drugs.

I am not totally against rehab. I know it works for some people. You have to want it to get it, and truthfully, I don't want it. I can't tell a single person how I really feel for fear of being thrown in jail. Tell me how this is supposed to help me. I fucking hate the justice system in this country.

I hate that people just won't let me be comfortable. If opiates make me happy, why is it so wrong? Why is booze legal, and heroin not? All of this makes me so depressed; I really want to end my life. I have nothing to look forward to. I felt the best feeling in the world when I was high. Now I am told that I can never feel like that again. I may as well go to hell and burn for eternity.

Somehow I start to fall asleep, but suddenly I am worried that something's wrong with Eleanor. I go out and grab a phone and call Pete. Tomorrow is Sunday, and we are allowed to go to leave the facility with family to attend church. I tell him to pick me up at 8:00 am and bring Elle. "We don't have to go to church.

We'll go through a drive-through and get some breakfast and then go to a park and play with Elle."

"Are you sure you won't get caught?"

"No, it will be fine. I'll say we went to a Baptist church; their mass is like three hours long. We will have plenty of time."

"Okay. I'll be there at 8:00 am sharp with Eleanor to pick you up for 'church.'"

"Thanks, Pete. You are so good to me. What did I ever do to deserve you?"

"You don't, but you're the most fun person I know, and I'd rather hang out with you than be all by myself all day."

"I love you; give Elle a kiss good night for me."

"Love you too. I will. Good night."

I feel better after talking with Pete, knowing that I will see him and Eleanor tomorrow when I wake up. It makes going to bed a lot easier. I'm sure the Valium helped too.

The next morning is cold, but the sun is shining brightly. I'm awake by 5:00 am, but we can't leave our floor until 6:00 am, so I take a long shower and get all dolled up. I want to look hot for Jesse today. Today is Sunday, so we don't have any groups today, and I hope if I look good Jesse will want to hang out with me this afternoon and play Scrabble or something.

At six, I make my down to the smoke shack with a cup of coffee. It is a peaceful morning smoke; this early everyone is still getting showered and dressed, so I have the shack to myself. I look around at the graffiti on the walls. It's all inspirational, which I think is stupid. If you're going to deface property you should write something shocking, not uplifting.

I hear the door of the house open and shut and footsteps coming toward me. I don't bother to move from my corner in the shack to peek at who it is. Suddenly Jesse steps into the shack and asks for my lighter. I hand it over to him, and he sits right next to me. I start to clam up. I don't want to say anything stupid or lame, and my heart is racing. It has been a long time since a guy has made me feel so anxious.

What I want to do is kiss him right there and take him up to my room and have my way with him. Of course I don't. What if he pushes me off and says I am gross or something? Instead we sit in silence. I try to act nonchalant, with my legs crossed and holding my cigarette away from my face like movie stars used to do in old movies.

Then he looks at me and says in a quiet fast voice, "You are really pretty right now."

I look at him and smile, my face blushes, and I stutter out, "Thank you, Jesse." It is totally unlike Jesse to say something like that; he is a macho, funny guy. I don't know what to think. Maybe I heard him wrong, but it sure sounded like, "You're pretty right now." But it couldn't have been. Could it?

He stubs out his cigarette, says, "I'll see you around," and leaves me sitting there dumbfounded. What the hell did he mean by that? Does he like me? We both know we can't be together here—we would get kicked out. Now I regret not kissing him. It's probably the only time we will ever be alone together in here. That was my chance, and I missed it.

I decide I need a Valium, so I finish my cigarette and go up to my room. It is seven, and Erin is still asleep. I wake her up and remind her of what she told me yesterday when I slept past seven. She hurries out of bed and gathers up her clothes and toiletries to jump in the shower. She has to wait a while for the shower because Ally is in there, and she takes forever. God only know what that women is doing to herself in there; she never looks any different when she comes out.

While Erin waits to get in the shower, she and I lie on our beds and shoot the shit. Then Erin says, "I am thinking about leaving. I really miss my boyfriend, and I don't think I need any more treatment. I don't feel like drinking anymore, so if I leave I won't drink, and I'll go to AA meetings. No big deal."

I tell her, "It's your choice; you're here by your own free will, so you can leave anytime you want. If you're not getting anything out of the treatment, you should let someone else get your bed who will. I think you'll end up drinking, though."

"No, Anna, I won't. It's like now that I'm finished with withdrawals, I don't ever want to drink again and go through that."

"I wish I was like you. All I want to do is use."

Erin says, "Promise you won't tell anyone if I tell you something?"

"Yeah, I promise."

"I only came here because my boyfriend was mad at me for drinking too much, so I figured if I went to rehab he would not break up with me. So far it's worked. Yesterday on the phone he told me that he wants me to come home as soon as I can."

"Hey, I only came because my asshole probation officer won't let me go back on methadone, so I totally understand. If I was in your position I would leave too."

"Really? You don't think I am being dumb?"

"Not at all. But you're not going to tell any about our secret pills, are you?"

"No, no. I won't."

"Good, so if you do leave, when do you plan on doing it?"

"Not today. I am going to call my boyfriend and talk to him about it, and if he still not going to be mad at me, I will leave tomorrow."

I tell her good luck and grab one of my pills, and we both sit quietly thinking about our futures.

What I really think is this: Erin is way too codependent, and she will be drinking again within a week. I mean come on, she is using Valium in rehab, and she doesn't think she has a problem. She is still in denial, and you can't get sober until you realize that you have a problem.

Truthfully, I want her to leave so I know for sure she won't tell on me for buying that Valium from her. I know that it's mean, but if she isn't ready to get sober, then she is wasting her time here anyway. Sure, I am not ready to get clean either, but it's here or jail, and I pick here.

Lamare knocks on our door, and I go to open it. He says, "Someone is here for you, Anna."

"Okay. I'll be right down. Thank you."

I look at the clock. It says 7:30 am, and Pete is a half hour early. I run down the stairs and out the door. Pete is sitting in my car in the parking lot. I go up to him and ask, "How did you get my car?"

"Your aunt Debbie called me, and we moved your stuff out of your apartment, so I took your car and brought it to my dad's house. I hope you don't mind that I drove it to pick you up."

"Are you driving it to work and stuff?"

"Oh no, I am not doing that. I just thought you would want to be in your own car today."

"Well, sure I do, but you're early and I can't leave until eight. We are not supposed to have guests at the house until two in the afternoon when visiting hours start. Why don't you go to Hardees and pick me up two cinnamon buns and a hot ham and cheese with an orange juice? Then come back and pick me up."

Pete says, "Okay, I'll be back at eight on the dot."

"I'll be here," I say.

He drives off, and I go over to the smoke shack to wait until he gets back. He drives up at two minutes before eight, but I run into the house and sign out. By the time I am done with signing out I can leave.

As soon as I get in the car, Eleanor is on top of me kissing me all over and whining with excitement. I was afraid she would forget who I was, but she didn't. It feels so good to see her and Pete. I feel free for the first time in over two weeks. I really don't want this to end.

Pete pulls into a park. He picked this one because it's just outside of the city and there is no chance anyone would drive by and see that I am not in church. I let Elle out of the car, and she stays right next to me, never looking away, like she's afraid I will disappear again. We sit down at a picnic table to eat. Elle sits on my lap, and I give her a few pieces of ham.

Pete and I don't say much. I don't want to tell him about Jesse, and it's against the rules to talk about what goes on in group. I am not one who follows the rules much, but Pete is not interested in gossip anyhow. There is nothing that I can say to him that I have not already said. He knows that I really want to spend time with my dog. So he just watches me play with Elle.

After we finish eating, we all go for a walk down the trail into the woods. Elle sticks right by us, only walking over to sniff something every now and then. I feel uncomfortable in silence, and when

I get uncomfortable I start to ask questions. I ask, "How is work going?"

"It's going fine, but can we not talk about work? I hate work and don't want to think about it if I don't have to."

"Sorry, Pete. Well, is there anything new with you then?"

"Well, I might be moving down to Florida by my mom, with my friend Chad. There is a lot of construction work down there, and I need to get out of Wisconsin."

"So that means we are totally over."

"Anna, you're the one who broke up with me, over two months ago. I have to move on, and right now we are not good for each other."

"What's that supposed to mean—we are not good for each other?"

"Look at where you are, Anna. Look at what you're doing to yourself."

"Fuck you, Pete. You knew when I first met you that I wanted to use heroin. I told you that my only goal in life was to be a junkie, and you fell in love anyway."

"Yes, you did, but I did not know how much it would hurt me to watch you slowly kill yourself. I still love you very much. I just think that you need to be alone at this point in your life, and so do I."

"So what the hell am I supposed to do when I get out of here? I don't have an apartment any more, no boyfriend now, no job, no dope. Fuck, Pete, I may as well kill myself. If it was not for my Eleanor and my mom and dad I really would, Pete."

"I know you would. You already are, Anna, and that's your choice, I know I am not going to change you. You have to do that on your own, or you don't. Either way I can't be around you right now."

I turn around and walk back toward the car, and I say, "Fine, you can be alone forever for all I care. Sorry I called you today and made you pick me up."

I get to the car and grab Pete's cell phone and dial my dealer's number.

He answers, "Who is this and what you need?"

"It's me, Anna. Can you bring me three methadone pills? Meet me at the county park."

"Okay, I'll be there in twenty minutes."

Pete and Elle come up behind me. I turn toward them and shut the door to the car. We all go back and sit at the picnic table. I tell Pete what I just did and ask to borrow fifteen bucks. He gives me the money and asks if he can have one of the methadone pills.

This is why Pete and I are bad for each other: he says he doesn't want me to use dope, but every time I get some, he uses it with me. He just never seeks out dope, so he thinks it's okay. I think in his mind he thinks, *She would get high one way or the other; I may as well pay for it and get high with her.*

I've known we are bad for each other for a year now, I just never said it out loud. I don't want to be alone. I still want him to love me, and only me, but I want him to give me my space to be with other guys and yet have him available so I can call him up if I need money or sex. Yet I still do love him; I am so confused.

My dealer pulls up. Pete hands me the money, and I go over to the dealer's car, give him the money, and take my pills from him. I go back over to the table and hand Pete his pill. I take one of mine and save the last one for later.

"Okay, Pete, I have calmed down. I understand that you need to leave Wisconsin. God knows I want to leave this God-forbidden state too. I just want to know if I can still call you and talk to you when you move."

"Of course, Anna. You can call me anytime you feel like it. I don't want to sever all contact or anything like that. I just want us to not be so dependent on each other."

"You know, Pete, I am keeping Eleanor. We will probably move up to Michigan with my dad after I get out of rehab."

"That's fine. I bought her for you. I expected you to take her. She loves you more anyway. At night she whines and sleeps on a one of your T-shirts you left at my dad's place that night you slept over."

This makes me very sad. I tell Pete, "I don't think I am going to make it through this program, I am going to end up back in jail. I can feel it in my bones. I'm so fucking scared of everything—getting clean, being alone, going to jail. I feel overwhelmed, and I want to skip out of this place, and I totally would if I had a way to get up to Michigan, but not in my car."

"Anna, what would you do when you get to Michigan? You will still be wanted by the police."

"By the police in Wisconsin, not in Michigan. I don't know what I would do for sure, maybe move down to Hawaii by my mom."

"Anna, I think you should stay in rehab, and if you become sure you're going to get kicked out, then call me. But do it at night when everyone is sleeping so we can get to Michigan before anyone knows you're missing."

"Okay, Pete, I will stay for now, but if I get even the slightest vibe that my counselor is going to call my PO then I am going to call you to pick me up."

As soon as I tell Pete how I really feel and know that he is willing to help me, I feel like the weight of the world has been lifted off my shoulders. That and the methadone pill I just took are starting to make me a little high, and I feel like I can do anything. Pete and I stay at the park for another half hour and play with Elle. Then we drive back to the rehab center. As I am getting out of the car Pete hands me a cell phone to use instead of having to use the house phone.

When I get back, I look around the whole house for Jesse, and there is no sign of him. I go to the living room and look at the sign-out sheet and find out that he signed out and went to church too. I didn't hear him say anything about someone picking him to go to church. Now I am really curious. In group he said his family lives in a different state, and he never mentioned any girlfriend.

The methadone makes me sleepy, so I go up to my room and read. I end up falling asleep.

When I wake up, it's already two in the afternoon, and visiting hours are starting. Almost everyone has a family member or friend at the house visiting. I make my way to the kitchen to make myself something to eat, and there is Jesse with a woman. She is pretty but a little chunky; not fat, just plump. I would guess she is in her early thirties, around Jesse's age. She is wearing a long flowing skirt with a tight sweater. She has an olive skin tone, blue eyes, and black curly hair down to her shoulders.

They are making a pizza to share. Jesse notices me walk in and introduces me to his woman friend. Her name is Lisa, and she is his ex-girlfriend. She says, "Hi," and goes back to what she was saying to Jesse. Jesse sort of gives me a look, as if to say sorry. I shake my head and smile, letting him know I don't mind.

I warm up some leftovers from last night's supper and go into the dining room and eat. One good thing about this place is that they make the best food. At night a resident assistant, or RA as we call them, comes in and makes dinner. The RAs also sleep here to make sure none of us leave or in case there is some kind of emergency. I guess that is why they sleep here, but I am not sure. Nobody ever really explained the RAs to me. The doors are not locked at night or anything, and the counselors are always telling us we can leave if we want to. Yet they have someone here at night to watch us. Sort of a mixed message.

I am still feeling "good" from the methadone I took this morning. Methadone makes me want to smoke. After I finish my food, I go outside and light up a cigarette. I notice that there is a new client. It is a man, about twenty or so. He has red hair and translucent skin. I go over and ask him what his drug of choice is. He looks gaunt and thin; I am guessing pills. I guess right on the mark—he is addicted to Oxycontin. Here in Green Bay it's hard to get heroin. You have to know people to get heroin, and those people go down to Chicago, Illinois, to pick it up. So most people in Green Bay who want an opiate fix get hooked on Oxys.

He tells me his name is Mark, but everyone calls him "Red." I tell Red, "I too am hooked on opiates; right now I am getting off methadone and coke. So I know how shitty you're probably feeling. I am not going to lie, Red. It sucks, but it gets a little better each day."

Red just sort of nods but doesn't say anything. I realize that I am a lot more talkative when I get some methadone in me. It's like I don't hate people as much when I am high. I decide to leave Red alone to be sick by himself. I know that when I'm dope-sick I don't want to talk either.

Two of the guys are playing "horse," and I walk over and grab the basketball and ask if I can play next round. Jesse is still in the house with his ex, and Erin is with her boyfriend in the basement. I don't want to go down there and disturb them. That is where people go to have sex. There is a little cubbyhole down there, and sometimes people sneak in it for a quick fuck. As far as I know, no one has gotten caught doing it the two times I have been here. I have never used it, but I thought about bringing Jesse down there for a quickie.

While I am playing horse, I notice that my body doesn't hurt at all. Ever since my third day in jail, my body has been aching. I realize how much better I feel when I have methadone in me, and it's not like I am super high or anything. I just have a buzz. It's like I am functioning at 100 percent again.

After I notice this, I get mad. I'm mad at the fact that I can't go back on methadone. At least not for seven months, when I am finally off of probation. I think about calling a lawyer and asking if it is even legal for my PO to keep me from seeking treatment at the methadone clinic. I really want to call a lawyer, but my parents already spent two grand on a lawyer when I first got into trouble. That lawyer is what kept me from possibly having to go to prison. Now that I fucked up the deal that lawyer made, I don't want to cost my parents another two grand just so I can get back on methadone.

My parent really want me to get clean. At least my dad does. Since my mom moved to Hawaii a year ago for a nursing job that was only supposed to last three months, I have not been talking with her too much. She was supposed to go down there to work and help pay off the new house she and dad built on a lake in upper Michigan. Then after three months she was supposed to come home and they would be retired. Instead my mom turned into a lush and a whore.

One night when I was up in Michigan visiting my dad while my mom is gone the phone rang. It was late at night, and my dad was already asleep, so I answered. It was my mom calling from Hawaii. There is a five-hour time difference, so it's not too late in Hawaii. She was drunk off her ass, and I could tell immediately that she was doing something stupid.

She said, "Anna, is that you?"

"Yes, Mom, it's me."

"Anna, is your dad awake?"

"No, Mom, it's almost midnight here. I was just about asleep too. Mom, I can tell you're pissed up. Is something wrong?"

"No, nothing is wrong, I just wanted to tell you that I am in love."

"What the fuck, Mom? Are you fucking crazy? You're married."

"I know, Anna, but your dad has always been so mean to me. Down here I am realizing that I don't need him anymore."

"Mom, how could you do this to Dad? He just lost his youngest daughter, and now you're leaving. You're going to kill him if you do this."

"Hey, I lost my youngest child too. Don't I have a right to have a life too? Anna, did you know your dad blames me for Angie's death?"

"No, Mom, he does not. He blames himself, and I blame myself. None of us have dealt with Angie's death properly. You're just drunk and not thinking right. You didn't have sex with anyone, did you?"

"Actually, Anna, yes I did."

"What the fuck, Mom? What were you thinking? You weren't thinking, were you?"

"Anna, I am sorry. I did not mean to hurt anyone, but it's my life."

"Yes, it is your life; so why do you have to tell me you're fucking someone else? It's not something you're supposed to tell your kid. Especially you kid who is a drug addict."

"I love you, Anna, and nothing will change that. Don't tell your father. I will tell him when I am ready. I have to go now. I love you, and be good."

Until that night I always thought I would not care if my parents were screwing around on each other, or even if they got a divorce. But after my mom told she was screwing around on my dad, I broke down. I was pissed off, sad, and scared. Just a few days before my mom gave me that call, my dad and I were eating dinner, and I asked him what he would do if Mom were to cheat on him. He said she never would do that, and he said that they had been married twenty-five years and nothing could come between their love. Holy shit, was he in for a shock!

I got that call from my mom in October, right before I went into rehab the first time. I did not say a word to my dad about it the whole time I was in rehab, but after I got kicked out and went to the methadone clinic, I was fed up with my mom. I wanted her to come home and take care of me, and I didn't want her to ever tell my dad what she did. So I called her one night right after I got kicked out of rehab and asked her to come home for Christmas and stay home. She said no, and we got into a fight.

I ended up telling my dad about my mom's infidelities right before Christmas. He was devastated. Since then my dad has been left to take care of me all by himself.

I don't want to call my dad and ask him to hire another lawyer just because I can't make it through thirty days of treatment. He has been through enough. His youngest daughter, my little sister, died three years ago in a car accident, his only living daughter is a heroin addict, in and out jail and rehab, and now his wife, the only stable part of his life, is cheating on him.

If I want to get out of here I'll have to do it without a lawyer. I'm going to have to take a chance and stay in this place and possibly get caught using drugs, or I can make a run for it and try to get to Hawaii to live with my mom and get back on methadone. My dad, did say once that he would like it if I went down to Hawaii and kept an eye on my mom. He figures if I was down there, she wouldn't be able to drink like a fish and fuck every barfly she comes across. At the time he suggested I move to Hawaii to keep an eye on my mom I was just starting the methadone treatment here in Green Bay and things were going good with my PO, so I did not want to move then and go through the rigmarole of getting my probation transferred to Hawaii and finding another methadone clinic in Hawaii. But now, if I can escape from this place without getting caught and make it to Hawaii, I would keep an eye on my mom and find a methadone clinic in Hawaii no problem. In my head I also think then maybe my parents would get back together and we would all live happily ever after. The whole problem with my being wanted in Wisconsin wouldn't be a problem if I was in Hawaii. Wisconsin wouldn't extradite me for a nonfelony; at least I don't think they would.

Visiting hours are done, and everyone's family and friends are gone. All of us dope fiends are getting ready for bed, even though it's only six in the evening. There is not much to do in rehab on a Sunday. We don't go to any AA meetings, so there is no reason to wear our going-out clothes. Everyone puts on sweat pants and T-shirts. I go down to the living room to watch some TV, and Jesse is down there. He asks me, "Would you go out to the smoke shack and have a cigarette with me?"

I say, "Sure. Let me just go up to my room and get a sweat shirt."

I run up to my room and put on a little makeup before I grab my sweater. I want to look good for him without him knowing that I am trying to look good for him. It's a hard balance to keep—not too much makeup, but just enough so I look like I have milky smooth skin.

When I look just right I go downstairs and make my way out to the smoke shack. I step into the shack, and he is already sitting down smoking. He motions for me to sit in the chair next to him. I feel very nervous. In my head I am wondering if he is going to try to kiss me, and now I wish I had rinsed my mouth out before I came down here. I sit down next to him and light my cigarette and ask, "So what did you want to talk about?"

He says, "Well, I just wanted to know if you think this place is working for you, or if you think you will use as soon as you get out."

"Well, do you want me to tell you the truth, or do you want to hear what I am supposed to say?"

"I want the truth. You know I am here because of my PO too, and if I get kicked out I also go to jail."

"The truth is, Jesse, that I don't want to get out of here and go back to using street drugs, but I do want to go back on the methadone treatment. As you know my PO said that I can't go back on the methadone as long as I am under his supervision. So truthfully I don't know what I am going to do when I get out of here. Why do you care?"

"Because, Anna, I like you, but I don't want to be with someone who is using."

Jesse, I like you too, and I think I sort of made that pretty obvious—maybe too obvious. The rules say that there are to be no sexual relationships in treatment, and if they even suspect a sexual relationship we can get discharged."

"Well, we are not having a sexual relationship, and I am getting released in four days. After that we can see each other."

"Actually, if you're on probation and I am on probation, we are not allowed to be in a relationship until we are off of the probation. I really do like you, and I really want to fuck you, but

I am not ready to be in a relationship right now, and I'm willing to bet you're not ready either, Jesse."

"So when I get out, you still have two weeks left in here. How about on Sundays I pick you up for church? Then we can have sex."

'Jesse, I am not sure I will even be here then. I could be in jail, or I might just take off. I can't believe that I am saying this to you. I have wanted to fuck you since I first saw you, and now here I am telling you I won't."

"You're probably right, Anna. We are not at the right point in our lives to be thinking about getting together. We should be focusing on staying clean. It's just that I am really attracted to you, and I really want to be with you."

"How about I give you my phone number, and we can keep in touch. Maybe someday when we get everything sorted out in our lives we can be together. Jesse, you have no idea how hard it is for me to do the right thing right now, because I really want to fuck."

"Me too. Me too."

Jesse takes the piece of paper with my number on it and stubs out his smoke and goes back into the house. I stay outside and light up another smoke. I need to take time and process what just happened.

I just met Jesse two days ago, and already I have to sort of break it off with him. I know I am doing the right thing for me. I don't need another man in my life, especially one with a coke addiction. The last thing I want is to start using that shit again. I sort of wish I could have gotten laid at least. If I had let that happen, I would have ended up falling in love or something and my life would be even more complicated than it already is. I reassure myself that I did the right thing, and I even feel proud of myself for not letting my loins make the decision for me.

I decide to go up to my room and lie down. When I get up there I notice that Erin's stuff is gone. Then I see the note lying on my bed. It says, "Dear Anna, I really didn't get to know you that well, but what I did know, I liked. I decided to leave with my boyfriend tonight. I did not tell anyone that I left, so when you get this note, you should bring down to the RA on duty, so they know you had nothing to do with my departure. Thank you, Erin."

I go down to the RA and hand him the note. He tells me to go up to my room and take her sheets and bedspread off her bed and put them in the washing machine. He goes into the office and makes some calls. I assume that the thing that really makes the staff mad when someone takes off without telling them is the fact that they will most likely not get paid by the insurance. I doubt they think it's their fault that an alcoholic is on their way back to the bottle. If they had any real addict staff at this place I think they would take the loss of a client a little harder.

I do as I am told and strip her bed and bring it all down to the wash. Alley comes out of her room and starts to ask me all kind of questions about Erin. I tell her I am too sad about her leaving to talk about it, but I am sure we will talk about it in issues group tomorrow. She gives me a hug and tells me not to let it affect my sobriety. Really I could care less that she left; I just don't feel like talking to Alley about it.

Tonight I have the room all to myself. I set my alarm for six in the morning and pull out my true crime novel and read. But I am unable to read, so I turn out the lights and grab a Valium to help me sleep. Then I look out the window thinking about the day's events and reminding myself how thankful I am to be in such a comfortable bed and able to look out a window and pass the time until I fall asleep.

The next morning is the same as every other morning in rehab. I get ready, I smoke, I eat, I smoke again, and I go into morning meditation. On this morning something is different. I can feel it in my bones as soon as I walk into the group room for morning meditation. As we are all sitting listening to instrumental music and trying to relax, most people have their eyes closed. Not me. I like to look out the window to relax, and as I am looking out the window I notice two police cars pull into the parking lot. My heart sinks into my stomach. I know they are here for me. I figure they have found my stash of Valium, or it could be any number of things I have done since I've been in rehab.

Jesse is sitting next to me, and I nudge him to make him look out the window and see the police cars. He does, and he whispers, "Who do you think they're here for, you or me?" I shrug my shoulders. Deep down I know they are here for me.

Just as that thought goes through my head, I see my probation officer walking up the steps to the rehab house. Jesse sees him too. At the same time we say, "My probation officer is here; it's me." I look at him, confused, and he looks at me the same way.

It takes a second to register in both of our brains that we have the same PO. There are five more minutes left of meditation, and we can't leave until the exact time is up. If we were to leave earlier, we would face being discharged. Even though we know that one of us is on our way to jail, neither of us get up to leave. We don't want to risk both of us going to jail this morning for something as stupid as leaving group early without permission.

Sitting in that room for those five minutes was the most intense five minutes I have ever sat through. Finally it's up, and we both run out of the room. I go and look out all the windows on the second floor, checking to see if there is any way I would be able run from here without getting caught. I notice that there are two police cars parked on both sides of the house to ensure that whoever it is getting picked up does not try to run. When I see that I have no way out, I go to my room, set my stuff on my bed, say a quick prayer, and head down the stairs. The entire walk down the stairs I'm thinking of how I'm going to get the cop's gun away from him and shoot myself in the head with it. I know I won't be able to last seven months in jail. I have to end it all right now, fast and painless.

I get to the bottom of the stairs and open the door to the first floor. First thing I see is my PO. I look at him, but he doesn't seem notice me. Then I see the police officer taking out his handcuffs; he doesn't seem notice me either. Finally I realize what's happening. It's Jesse who is going to jail, not me. I can't believe it, I feel relieved for a moment, but then the realization that I probably will never see Jesse sets in and I am overcome with sadness. What had Jesse done to get kicked out of rehab and put in jail? The only thing I can think of was the other day when he was late for assignment group, and he was written up. I had no idea that was his third time being written up that day. How could the counselors do this to him, for being a couple of seconds late to group!? Anger boils up in me like I have never felt before. How could this place be so merciless? He is suffering with an addiction, and he was in a place that is supposed to help him overcome this addiction, but instead of helping him they are punishing him, and for something so fucking trivial.

My PO notices that I'm just standing there watching Jesse being hauled away, and he tells me to go back to where I'm supposed to be. I can feel my face redden with anger. I want to lash out at him. I can feel the hairs on my neck stand up, but I do nothing. I just walk away and go out the back door to the smoke shack. I don't speak to anyone. I just light my cigarette and cry. I am so thankful that it wasn't me being taken off to jail, although after seeing what just happened to Jesse I'm even more fearful that my turn is next. If he can be kicked out for such a meaningless offense there is no way I will make twenty-five more days in this place and not go back to jail. I know right then and there I have to escape from this place and make my way up to Michigan by my dad.

The rest of the day goes by slowly. In issues group that morning we had to "process" Jesse's arrest. I should have received an Emmy for my performance in that group. I fed the counselors with all the bullshit they wanted to hear me say, like how I understand that Jesse didn't follow the rules and that he needed to go to jail to learn that in life there are rules. All the while I'm saying these things, I'm thinking of how I am going to make my escape.

That night, at our AA meeting, I call Pete and tell him that I'm for sure breaking out of rehab and going up to Michigan. I tell him not tonight, but tomorrow after lights out, he should meet me at the Village Inn motel across the street from the rehab.

After the AA meeting, we all go back to the house and get ready for bed. I go up to my room and begin to write a letter to Jesse. I say nothing of my plan to escape, knowing that I have to send this letter to the jail and that all the mail in jail is read by guards before the inmate gets it. In the letter I tell him to keep his hopes up, that he will be out soon enough, and when he is out I will be waiting to see him again. I send him my phone number again, because I'm sure that when the counselors pack his room they won't give him the piece of paper with my number on it I had given him earlier.

For the rest of the night I plan my escape down to every last detail. I am not going to tell my dad that I'm coming. The less everyone knows what I'm going to do the better. I'm not going to pack all my belongings I have here in rehab. I will just take the essentials; the rest they can throw away. I sit in my bed going over every detail I can think of and trying not to think about what will happen if something goes wrong. Before I know it, it's two in the morning and I am wide awake. I get up and go under my bed where I have the Valium hidden. I take four out and eat them. Right now I just need to be out of it for a little while. Within a half hour I'm sound asleep.

The next morning, it's business as usual. No Jesse, no fun, and no changes being made in my life. I have no desire to stay in rehab or get clean. I don't even bother to shower or change my clothes today. I'm a mess. I am terrified that at any moment the police and my probation officer will be at the door to take me back to jail. I still plan on escaping, but in the light of day my plan doesn't seem so promising. At least I know I can always count on Pete. He and Eleanor are the only things that are keeping me going today.

We do our routine—groups and more groups. In each group I'm in today I am questioned about what's wrong. I look at them and say, "Oh nothing. I'm just having a bad day." I'm not even so sure what is wrong. Sure I have the threat of jail looming over my every second and the thoughts of killing myself rolling over and over in my head, but I have those all the time. Today isn't much different. Today there is no Jesse; there is no life. I feel like I'm not a part of anything, not even my family. I miss my parents so much, and my mom is almost on the other side of the earth. I want my parents to get back together. If I could just make it to Hawaii and give my mom a good shaking, show her how she is fucking up not only her life but the lives of all those she loves most, maybe then Mom and Dad will live and love together.

I go out for a smoke, and Ally comes up to me. The last thing I want to do is talk to her today. She starts going on and on about the AA meeting tonight. She is saying something about being attracted to a guy at this particular meeting. I am smoking my cigarette trying to stay calm while I listen to her go on and on. For some reason, though, I just can't. Ally represents everything

I hate about rehab. She thinks this place is some sort of magic answer to her drug problem. She has this illusion that as soon as she is out of rehab, her life will be the most amazing productive life anyone has ever led. I have seen her type before, the last time I was in rehab. She has what is called a rehab high, when the idea of staying clean seems so easy because you're in a "safe place" where the outside world can't tempt you with its feminine wiles. Everyone I've seen who has had this rehab high has crashed and gone right back to the drug.

I can feel my legs getting stiff. I can feel myself get up, but I don't realize what I'm about to do. I stand up and scream, "Shut the fuck up! You're a junkie, and you will always be a junkie. You're no different from any one of us. We all have the same slim odds of actually staying clean outside of this place."

After I say it, I immediately feel bad, and I apologize. I tell her that I'm just having a rough time today and I didn't mean a single word I just said. I do mean it, but I take it back anyway. I don't want to get kicked out for saying I don't think Ally will stay clean. Ally doesn't seem too shook up about my outburst; as soon as I'm done apologizing she is right back to her motor-mouthing about this guy in AA. I run into the house as fast as I can and up the stairs to my room. I pick up my phone and call Pete. It's 3:00 pm, and tonight is the big night. I am blowing this joint.

Pete answers the phone, and he sounds out of breath. I ask, "What were you doing, jacking off?"

He says, "No, Anna, but thanks for asking."

I go on to say, "Well, Pete, tonight's the night. Are you ready?"

"Yup, I sure am. Are you?"

I say, "I don't know. I just blew up outside at one of the other house guests. I can't get my mind off the fact that I could end up in jail for seven months at any moment, and I have no idea how I'm going to get out of this damn place without being noticed."

Pete says, "Anna, calm the fuck down. I will be there no matter what happens. I love you. I will be waiting for you at 11:00 pm in the Village Inn parking lot. We can do this."

This makes me feel a little better, He says, "I think you should take a few of your Valium and just relax. You can't let people know you're up to anything."

"You're right, Pete. I will take a few Valium and go to this AA meeting like I normally would. I will act as normal as I can without seeming suspicious. I've got go now. I will see you in a few hours. I love you too. Thank you, Pete, for doing this for me. I don't know what I would do without you."

He says, "I don't know what you would do without me either, but you're going to have to figure that out pretty soon, because I'm moving to Florida for sure."

I say, "I can't talk about that right now, but whatever, I love you and bye."

"Bye, Anna, and don't worry. It will happen how it's supposed to happen."

I get off the phone and immediately take three Valium as Pete suggested. Then I sit and read through the journals of Kurt Cobain until it's time to go to AA.

After those Valium kicked in the afternoon goes by fast. Before I know it, it's 10:00 pm and everyone is getting ready for bed. The RA who is on tonight is the old lady with bad hearing. I lucked out so far. I don't have a roommate, so I just might get out of here undetected. I go about my business as if I too am just getting ready for bed as I do every night in here.

I think about Jesse for a minute, and it seems like such a long time ago that he was in here with me. It's only been one full day, but it seems like eons ago. I still haven't been able to process his leaving properly. I think to myself, as soon as I'm out of this place I will make sure to write him a letter in jail. I can't put my name on it, but he will figure out it's from me. Hopefully.

At 11:00 pm I throw as much shit as I can into one duffel bag. I have to leave a few items behind. The most missed will be the journals of Kurt Cobain, but I don't have time to think about it. I pack fast and hard. I get as much as I can in. I am finished at 11:11 pm. I make a wish on the clock. I can't say it or it won't come true. I think you can guess it. At 11:00 pm is lights out, so all the lights are out. I walk as quietly as I can down the hallway. The RA is downstairs on the first floor in the office. I just have to make it down a half a flight of stairs in the house and out the fire escape and across the parking lot and road and I'm free.

I make it outside to the fire escape and shut the door behind me. I cringe as I shut it, because it's loud. As soon as the door is shut, I take off down the stairs like a bat out of hell. The only thought I have is to run. I run as fast as my feet will allow. I make it to the road, but I don't see Pete's car. I panic and run across the road. I keep looking back to see if anyone is looking for me. I see a cop drive by, and I duck into the lobby of the Village Inn. I ask how much a room is, to make it seem like I have a reason to be in there aside from running away from rehab. I don't pay attention to the answer. I just look for Pete. I pull out my phone and call him. He answers on the fourth ring, just as I'm about to hang up.

I say, "Where the fuck are you? You're supposed to be here. I am here, and you're not. Are you coming?

Pete says, "Sorry. I fell asleep. I am on my way right now."

I say, "Hurry up," and I hang up.

Pete lives about eight minutes away. Each second I wait for him, I get more and more nervous. By the time he pulls up I'm in a full-blown panic attack. I see his car and run out of the lobby and into his car.

I say, "Thank God. Drive."

He says, "There is a problem. I don't have enough gas to take you all the way to Michigan, and I don't have any money."

I say, "Shit."

I call my dad and tell him that I skipped out of rehab. He's asleep when I call. I don't have time to tell him the whole story right now, so I tell him what he needs to know. I ask him if he will call my aunt Debbie and ask if I can sleep there until he can pick me up in the morning. He says, "Why don't you call her?"

"Because, Dad, it's almost midnight, and I would give her a heart attack."

Then I decide against going to Debbie's. She might be mad at me for skipping out and try to call them to take me back. It would be good intentions on her part, but I would end up in jail. I can't think of anyone else. I can't stay at Pete's because that's the first place my probation officer would look for me. Then the idea pops in to my head: my grandma Grace. I rarely see my grandma. We are not very close with my mom's side of the family. I call her and tell her that I was kicked out of rehab in the middle of the night and I have no place else to go. I can tell she is surprised and worried. I just woke my eighty-year-old grandma who just lost her husband in the middle of the night and asked her if I can hide out at her place until my dad gets me in the morning.

She says yes. I knew she would. I really didn't want to have to go there, but she is my last resort. No one would ever think I would go there. Not even my dad. I have to call him and tell him that's where I will be when he picks me up.

My grandma lives in Spruce, which is about fifty miles north of the rehab. It's two counties away, which is good. Pete has just enough gas to get me there and get himself home. After I know for sure that I have a place to stay for the night that is semi-safe and I know that my dad will be there as soon as he can, I feel a little bit better. Still, every time we pass a cop on the way to my grandma's house my heart jumps into my throat. I keep telling Pete, "Make sure you're not speeding. That's the last thing I need right now." He does fifty-five all the way there, even on the freeway where the speed limit is sixty-five.

I had been so worried I hadn't even noticed Eleanor in the car. I have my baby back. We will be sleeping together at my grandma's house tonight. By tomorrow I will be in Michigan with my dad. I will have an unlimited supply of morphine, as long as I can find it. I know he will be watching me closely, so I have to be sneaky when I look for it.

Pete pulls into my grandma's driveway. I look at him, and he looks at me. Then in the most sincere voice I ever heard Pete use, he says, "Anna, I love you. Call me when you're settled." I tell him I love him, and then I grab my bag, and Eleanor, and get out. I walk up to the door. All the lights are on in the house. Grandma is up. It's 12:30 am, and her outlaw granddaughter is coming to hide out.

I knock, and she comes to the door. Pete pulls out of the driveway when he sees me go inside. I wave and blow a kiss. I walk inside, and immediately I feel uncomfortable. What am I going to say? How am I going to explain this? Thank God for Eleanor. I have to take her outside to go to the bathroom. I use this as an excuse to not have to tell Grandma the whole story.

I take Eleanor out, and I then I sit with Grandma. She doesn't ask too much. She just asks about my mom. She has been worried about her. She has heard about the split with my dad. My mom doesn't talk to Grandma very often. I'm not sure why that is, but I think it's because my grandma is a quiet person. I answer Grandma's questions, and she tells me that she has heard about my problems too and that she has been very worried about me. I feel so bad. How could I do this to my sweet grandma? I love her and have always wished we had a closer relationship. The whole time I'm talking with Grandma I keep hating myself more and more for dragging her into this. I leave out the fact that I'm wanted by the police and could possibly be picked by the cops at any moment and brought to jail. If that happened in front of her, it would kill her. I have to be careful. I ask Grandma if I can use her phone. My dad told me to call him as soon as I got to Grandma's house. He wanted to make sure I'm safe. He is still digesting all this. I call, and he says he should be there by noon tomorrow. He is going to go back to bed, and he will leave in the early morning. It's a four-hour drive, so he should sleep.

After I get off the phone with my dad, Grandma says she is tired and is going to bed. I say good night. I take Eleanor and go upstairs to my mom's old room. When my sister and I slept here when we were little, we used to be so very scared of the upstairs. My mom used to tell us that it was haunted. Tonight, though, I could care less if it's haunted up there. I'm just glad to be out of rehab. As soon as I lay my head down Eleanor and I are asleep.

The next morning I wake early. There is no clock, I can only tell it's early by the sky. It's pink and blue and white. I go to look out the bedroom window to think through what went on last night, what my future may hold.

I can hear my grandma rustling downstairs, putting on coffee. Ever since I can remember my grandma's gotten up early. I don't want to go down there and face her; I don't want to go down to reality yet. I want to stay up here in my mother's childhood bedroom and make believe that my sister is still alive and that my parents are sleeping in the other room because we are all visiting Grandma for a vacation. Eleanor lies on my lap, and suddenly I'm brought back to reality. I'm a fugitive, and I've brought my unwitting grandmother into the situation. I begin to cry. I love my dog so much, and without her I would have ended this life of mine long ago with just one bullet to my drug-addled brain.

I know Eleanor has to go outside to go potty, so I take her. I slide out the door before my grandma could even notice I am downstairs. My grandma lives in the country. There is pond in the front yard, with a sun house next to it. The driveway is long and wide. The house is brick and is exactly as I remember it from childhood—even the smell. It's early spring, and it's a warm day. The odor of the ground thawing is overwhelming. I watch as Eleanor goes over to the backyard, near the path to the woods, to go potty. I follow her over there as she smells and runs.

I want to be lost in my head. Every time I've been put in mental hospitals for suicidal behavior, I've always used my grandma's house as my mental escape. It's beautiful here. It's quiet and private. There are good memories everywhere I look, mostly memories of my sister and me as children playing house in the woods by the stream; jumping over the stream and missing the landing and walking back to the house soaking wet from falling into the stream; Grandma scolding us, but making hot chocolate, and giving us warm towels to dry us off; Grandpa always outside fixing something. Always when I escape into my head to my grandma's house, the song "Strawberry Fields" by the Beatles is playing. For whatever reason, I associate that song with happiness.

I know I have to go into the house and explain to my grandmother what's going on. How can I do with this without my helper heroin? I take Eleanor inside, and Grandma has made up some meat for Eleanor for breakfast. She has coffee and peanut butter toast made for me.

She says, "I thought you'd sleep in today, after the night you had last night."

I say, "Oh no, I can't sleep in anymore. In rehab we had to be up at 6:00 am, and, well, now it's just second nature to me."

She looks at me with concern in her eyes, and I can tell I need to tell her something. But I can't possibly tell her the truth. It would break her fragile heart. Her granddaughter is a drug addict who just snuck of rehab and is now wanted by the police because of it. No, there's no way I can tell the truth.

Instead, I tell her, "Last night I left my light on past 11:00 pm, and since it was my third strike I was kicked out."

She asks, "So what are your plans now?"

I explain, "Well, my dad said he'd be here around noon to pick me up. I'm going to go stay by him for a while, until I can get a ticket to Hawaii to stay with my mom and get away from the drugs."

She says, "Well, I hope it all works out, but I have to run into town and get some face cream and groceries. Would you mind coming with me, and we'll have lunch at the diner? I'll have you back before noon."

"That sounds like a great morning, Grandma. I'll just go and get dressed and we can be on our way."

I go back upstairs and rummage through the one duffel bag I took in my rehab breakout to find something to wear. This is when I realize how much I actually left behind. I only have about ten things in this duffel bag, and I had at least thirty things at rehab. I don't mind—it's just stuff. If I had taken the time to pack all of it, I wouldn't get to see it or use it anyway, because I'd be in jail.

I find a suitable outfit, and Eleanor and I go downstairs. I put Eleanor in her bag, and we are off to town.

While in town, my hometown, we drive past everything that seems like home to me. There's the beach; there's the bank and the gas station. I want to ask her to drive past our old house, the one we lived in before Angie died, but I don't. Grandma runs her errands, and I sit around and watch, playing with Eleanor, just happy to be free.

When we get back we have a half hour before my dad gets there. I remember that my grandma had breast cancer, and she had surgery for it. Which mean that she probably has pain pills. I remember where Grandma keeps her pills. So when Grandma goes to use the bathroom, I go into the kitchen and look in the cupboard. Sure enough, there's a bottle of Percocet. I take a handful and eat two then and there and put the rest in my pocket.

I know as soon as I leave my grandma will check the cupboard where she keeps her pills and find that I took some of her pain pills. She will be disappointed, but she will never call me out or tell anyone.

Ten minutes after I take the two Percocets, I begin to feel a lot better. Actually, I feel much less depressed. I strike up a conversation with my grandma, who is one of the quietest people I know. I ask about our ancestry and about Ireland. She answers me as best she can, and suddenly my dad pulls into the driveway.

My dad won't come into my grandma's house, because since the split between my parents my dad doesn't like my grandma, so I had my stuff already downstairs and ready to go. I just grab

Eleanor and give grandma a hug bye and say thank you and I love you, and I'm off.

With the Percocets running through my blood steam I'm comfortable for the first time in over a month. Sure, I used in rehab, but I was always nervous I'd be found out and hauled off to jail. This time I can just relax and let the effects of euphoria take over.

I jump into the jeep and say, "Hello," to Dad. Right away, even before we've pulled out of the driveway, I'm spilling my guts to him about why I'm not in rehab, telling him half truths and leaving out the parts that make me look like I'm still a full-blown addict. I've hurt my dad in so many ways, and I can only tell him certain parts of why I left rehab and risked going back to jail for seven months. I can't tell him that I want to stay on opiates for the rest of my life. That the only peace I find comes from a poppy plant.

It feels so good to see my father's face and smell his smell. Eleanor is jumping all over him, licking his face. She loves my dad just as much as she loves me. Ever since I've been stealing my dad's morphine and bringing Elle up to Michigan with me, she has fallen in love with my dad. My dad loves her back just as much. I have the Percocets with me, and knowing those pills are in my pocket gives me a feeling of confidence and security. We have a four and a half hour drive ahead of us, but I'm on my way to freedom, and four hours doesn't seem like long to wait when I've been waiting for a month or so.

The first half of the drive up to Michigan we talk nonstop, filling each other in on what is new in our lives. The last half of the drive we sit comfortably silent. I can tell he is just relieved to have me with him so he can protect me. He won't have to worry about getting that knock on the door, the knock on the door he's already been through.

We stop at a gas station on the way up. I ask Dad to get me water, and I go into the bathroom. I take out the rest of the Percocets I took from my grandma; there are four left. I get greedy and take all of them. I want to take away all the anxiety, pain, and fear I have from being on the run. I know that my dad has his morphine at home in Michigan. I'm sure he hid it, but I always find it. He used to put it in a safe, but I figured out the combination. We are only an hour away from home now; these four pills should tide me over until I can find his stash.

When I get back out to the truck, my dad says, "Your phone rang while you were in the bathroom."

I ask, "Did you answer it?"

He says, "No. Should I have?"

"Absolutely not," I say.

I look at my caller ID, and it says private caller. I know exactly who that is. Nobody else I know uses private caller when calling besides him—my probation officer. It's almost 3:00 pm. I've been gone from the Jackie Nitschke Center rehab program for eleven or so hours now, and he's just now trying to get in touch with me. I figure this means that the staff at the rehab didn't notice I was gone until morning group. I wonder if my probation officer thinks I'm stupid enough to answer a private number. I wonder if he thinks I'm stupid enough to stay in the state. He knows that both my parents live out of the state, so he's probably smart enough to realize that I'm long gone by now. He can't put out a felony warrant against me, because my lawyer made sure I pled out to a misdemeanor possession. This means he can't cross state lines to find me. Even so, Michigan isn't far enough away from Wisconsin. I have to get down to Hawaii.

Then I remember I don't have any ID. My probation officer kept it until I was done with rehab. I can't get a plane ticket without an ID. I'm going to have to go to the DMV in Michigan and get a Michigan ID. That's going to take time; I have to send in my birth certificate and then wait up to two weeks before I can get my official Michigan ID card, which I need to book my flight.

I have so much running through my mind. Not even the four Percocets I took are keeping me from spinning around in my head. My biggest fear is going back to jail. My mind isn't strong enough to spend seven months in a county jail.

After four hours, we pull into the driveway of my parent's log cabin home. They just built this place less than two years ago. It is huge and right on the shore of Lake Gogebic. My dad retired early from his job at Georgia Pacific Paper Mill due to a severe back injury he received during hand-to-hand combat in the military. His back was broken. Now he gets 100 percent disability from the veterans as well as Social Security.

Oh yes, and today is my dad's fiftieth birthday. It's probably his worst birthday in his entire fifty years. His daughter just escaped from rehab and is addicted to heroin and opiate pills. His wife of twenty-five years is living in Hawaii, fooling around on him. His other daughter is dead. Since I've been gone, and my mom has been gone, my dad lives in this huge log cabin all by himself. The cabin is so big, and there are so many windows overlooking the lake, that the house is hard to heat. They have some kind of under-the-floor heating, but after they laid down the hardwood flooring the floor heating didn't work so well, so he mostly uses the fireplace and space heaters. The lake my dad's cabin is on is very remote. Not many people live there year-round. There is a bar up the road a mile or two. In the winter the bar is mostly full of tourists up in the north woods for snowmobiling. Once the snow melts though, there is no one around for miles.

To keep my dad company up there in the woods, he has two dogs. Both the dogs used to be mine. They are both mutts. I got Shawnee when I was in eighth grade, and I got Shasta when I was eighteen and living with my high school sweetheart. Dad also has two horses that he loves dearly. They are pulling horses.

I remember when Angie and I were still in middle school. Every summer just before school started there was the Gillett Fair, and every year at the Gillett Fair there was the horse pulls. Every year Dad would take me and my sister. I remember feeling bad for those horses being made to pull all that weight. Still, I went every year because it made my father happy. Ever since Angie died, we haven't gone to watch the horse pulls at the Gillett Fair. In fact, ever since Angie died, my parents rarely go back to our hometown. They sold the house we grew up in. They said they couldn't bear to live in the home Angie was raised in, in the city where she was raised. There were too many reminders of Angie, and they saw her tragic death everywhere they looked. Also, my dad blamed the Oconto Falls paramedics for my sister's death. We all had to find someone, or something, to blame it on.

I blamed it on myself. If only I had stayed home that night, instead of driving up to Michigan to steal some of my dad's pills. Angie and I were supposed to drive up to see my parents the next day, but I had to go that day, because I wanted to get my hands on those pills. At that point I don't think I realized I was hooked.

If only I had stayed home, she wouldn't have had the party at the house, and she never would have driven drunk down County Road. I could have saved her. After Angie died, my parents used up my dad's retirement fund from Georgia Pacific to build this beautiful log cabin, my parents' dream home. That cabin broke them. Money was short, and my mom needed to go back to work to make ends meet.

Then my mom went to Hawaii as a traveling nurse to make some extra money to help pay the mortgage. Instead she started drinking every night and sleeping around with men from the bar she frequented. So my dad was left to deal with me, his only living child; the child who is slowly killing herself as he stands by and watches, helpless do anything. I can tell I'm killing him little by little with my addiction.

What I can't understand is that my dad has a valid reason to get fucked up every day on pain pills. He has every reason in the world to get high off those pills, but he doesn't. He only takes them when he needs them. So he always has lots of pills. The doctor overprescribed, and he has so many pills that he never notices if I take fifty or sixty of them at one time.

When we walk in the house, we are greeted by Shawnee and Shasta. Eleanor clings to me. She doesn't like big dogs. She's been up here before with Shawnee and Shasta, and it always takes a day or two before she is comfortable with them. I carry her around with me. My dad lights a fire right away. It's already 5:00 pm and just getting dark. It's cold in this big house, especially at night.

My bedroom is upstairs. It's a huge loft, half the size of the house. On one side of the loft is Angie's old bedroom set, and on the other side is my bedroom set. In the middle of the loft there is a couch. When you sit on that couch, you look straight out a giant picture window overlooking the lake. It's beautiful to watch the sun go down up in this loft bedroom.

As soon as I have all my shit in the house and have Eleanor settled down, I begin to think of where I should start to look for my dad's stash of morphine. They are probably in his room. Dad and I sit down to watch TV, but the entire time we are in the living room, instead of watching the show, I'm contemplating how I'm going to get my hands on enough morphine to keep balanced until I can make it to Hawaii and get back on methadone treatment.

My dad stands up and goes into the bathroom. I'm hoping this is my moment. I hope he has to take a shit. As soon as he shuts the door to the bathroom I jump up and run into his room on my tiptoes. There they are—huge bottles of morphine. All I can find is the 15 mg bottles. I want the 30 mg, but beggars can't be choosers. So as fast as I can I open the bottle and pour out a handful of pills. I have no place to hide them, so I have my fist clenched. I hear my dad flush. I have to hurry. I hear the door open, and as he walks out of the bathroom, he sees me running out of his room. Right away he asks, "What's in your hands?"

I say, "Nothing," scared shitless.

I can see his face contort the way it does when he is really fucking pissed off. He tears my hands open, and a bunch of blue pills fall all over the floors. I bend down to pick them up so the dogs doesn't get to them. I hear my dad screaming at me.

He screams, "You worthless piece of shit. You can't even go one fucking day without putting that shit in your veins."

By now I'm crying and saying, "Sorry, Dad. I'm so sorry, Dad. I know I'm worthless."

Then he says, "I don't know what I'm going to do with you. You need to be in that rehab. I'm calling the police and telling them where you are."

I scream, "No, Dad. They're not going to put me back in rehab; they are going to put me back in jail. Please, Dad, don't call the cops."

I pick up all the pills I see and hand them over to my dad. He tears them out of my hands and storms off into his room with the phone.

I had managed to keep three 15 mg morphine pills without him noticing. I go up to the loft and pull out my works. I always have a works kit stuffed someplace no one would ever look in my room. As fast as I can, I cook up those three morphine pills and put them in my syringe and inject them. I feel the initial high. It feels good. Then I lie down and listen to my dad on the phone. He's talking about cops to someone.

Now that I have the opiates in my bloodstream, I have calmed down. I know what I have to do. I bring Eleanor up in the bed with me. I grab a pen and paper. I go downstairs and grab a bottle of five hundred aspirin 325 mgs. I find a bottle of wine in the fridge. I go back upstairs and begin taking handful after handful of the aspirin, swallowing them down with my wine chaser. As I write the note, I am calm. I feel like I can finally think clearly. I know that this is what I need to do. I can't put my father through this shit anymore. I am worthless, a junkie, a whore. I can't live without opiates, or really I don't want to live without opiates. I can't go back to jail. I can't. I write out three different notes: one to my dad, one to my mom, and one to Peter.

By the time I am done writing the notes, I have taken the entire bottle of aspirin. It's been an hour, and my dad comes up to see if I am high. I just lie there in my bed with Eleanor and don't say a word to him. He can read it all when I'm gone, but he keeps prodding me about how I'm doing. I just tell him, "I'm sorry," and that I'm tired from the past two days' events. I just want to sleep. He goes back down to his room. I didn't even bother to ask if he really did call the police on me. I just lay down, petted Eleanor, and kept telling her I'm sorry, but my dad can take better care of you than I can. I cry to Eleanor until I fall asleep.

The next thing I remember is waking up in a hospital. Everything floods back, and I remember why I'm here. I'm irate. I wanted to die. I want to be dead. Why am I alive? I call the nurse and tell her I'm sore and I need something take the pain away. She gives me some IV Demerol. I ask her what happened and where my dad is. She says to me, "Wait a minutes. I'll go get the doctor, and he can tell you." Then I notice that there is some woman sitting in my room. I ask her why she is in my room, and she answers back, "To make sure you don't try to kill yourself again."

A hour passes, and finally the doctor comes into my room. My ears are ringing, and I'm too weak to stand. The doctor starts to tell me that I was found by my father unresponsive in my bed.

"He called 911, and by the time we got there you no longer had a pulse. The EMTs administered CPR and got a pulse. You were airlifted by helicopter to Marquette Michigan hospital. When you got here, your kidneys were failing and your heart was beating erratically. We had to give you dialysis to get the aspirin out of your body and try to stabilize you."

I ask, "Where is my dad?" He is still in Iron Wood, Michigan. I begin to cry at the thought of my dad finding me almost lifeless, waiting for an ambulance to come get me. All of this on his fiftieth birthday. Just thinking about how selfish I had been and am makes me want to die even more.

The doctor then gives me some papers to sign for more dialysis treatments. I refuse to. He informs me that if I don't get my blood cleared of all the aspirin in it, I will die. I say good and try to throw the papers on the floor as hard as I can. But I am so weak that I can't even pick up my arm, so I have to push them off my bed. I tell the doctor to fuck off and let me die. After I say that, the doctor puts something into my IV, and it makes me fall asleep. A few hours later I wake up and I'm hooked up to a dialysis machine. I later found out that I was deemed too depressed and not in my right mind at the time, and therefore the doctors were able to give me the treatment I needed to stay alive.

I stay in the ICU for four days. Both my mom and my dad call, but I'm too weak to talk. I just sleep. Finally the ringing in my ears stops. When I tell the nurse this, she tells me that it's a good sign. Aspirin in large doses makes your ears ring, and that means that the aspirin is out of my bloodstream. I have blood taken every three or four hours when I'm in ICU, so I never get a restful sleep.

On the fifth day I am moved to a different part of the hospital until a psychiatrist comes down to see me. Every day while I'm in that hospital, the doctor comes in and asks, "Do you feel like killing yourself right now? And do you have a plan?"

I always answer, "Doesn't everyone think about killing themselves at some point or another? Yes, I have a plan to kill myself, but no, I'm not going to act on it any time soon."

On my sixth day I am transferred from the regular hospital to a mental ward. Every day my dad calls, and my mom calls once or twice. I don't have insurance, so they can only hold me for seventy-two hours. I was diagnosed as bipolar three years earlier, but I don't mention that to the psychiatrists. I figure that they might come up something totally different. I never admit to being an addict, which is hard because I have track marks up and down my arms. I just blame them on the doctors while I was in ICU. While in the psychiatric ward, I call the methadone clinics in Hawaii, on the island of Oahu, where my mom lives. I get their phone numbers and addresses, and I tell my dad on the phone that as soon as I get out of here, we are going to get my Michigan ID and then buy a plane ticket from Minnesota to Hawaii. He agrees. At this point I hate my mother, mainly for leaving my father alone in the middle of nowhere with one daughter dead only three years and the other daughter in the midst of a drug addiction and suicide attempt. I really do doubt that if I had died my mom would have come home for the funeral. Now I am going to live with her.

After my seventy-two-hour hold is up, my dad drives the three hours across upper Michigan to pick me up. He brings Eleanor. When he picks me up, we act as if nothing has happened. All I say is, "I'm sorry, Dad." We haven't spoken about it since. Still every time I think about my dad, I think about how he found his father dead of a suicide in our garage and he found his only living daughter almost dead in her bed upstairs in the loft.

I am not sent home with any good drugs, not even Valium. I did have an appointment with a doctor in Ironwood the next day, for x-rays of my kidneys. My dad drives me to that appointment to make sure I don't get any drugs. The mistake my dad makes is to wait in the waiting room for me. I give the doctor my usual spiel of HIV and pain, and he writes me out a scrip for methadone 60 mgs a day and a scrip for Valium 5 mgs twice daily. I know I couldn't get these scrips filled with my dad around, so I go to the hospital pharmacy and fill them and charge it to my hospital bill.

It has been over a month now since I last used methadone. My tolerance is low. All I need is 30 mgs of methadone and 10 mgs of Valium and I am as high as I have ever been injecting Dilaudid. Plus I have enough methadone and Valium to last me until I fly to Hawaii.

Part 2

Chapter 4

My Michigan ID comes in two weeks later, and my aunt Debbie buys the plane tickets that day over the Internet. Two days later we drive over to Duluth, Minnesota. Both my dad and I are nervous. I'm sad because I will be leaving my dog Eleanor behind with my father. My dad is nervous because he is sending me down to keep both me and my mom in line. He figures that if I am there my mom won't do so much sleeping around and I won't do so much smack.

We get in the ticket line. It is short, and a thin, blonde lady about thirty-five with thick red lipstick is going to be checking me into the airport. My dad has his hands in his pockets jingling his change around. It's something he does when he's nervous. I stand there in line with Eleanor in her bag over my shoulder, spending these last few precious moments with her. I have packed lightly, carrying all the summer clothes my mom told me to bring. I don't have much for summer clothes. She said we would go shopping when I got down there.

We get up to the lady with the bright red lips, and she asks for my ID. I give her my brand new Michigan ID. I put my luggage on the scale to weigh and to be taken away as I will not be carrying anything on with me except my purse. I have a nine-hour layover in Phoenix, Arizona. The main thing in my purse that I need is my methadone, Valium, cash, and phone.

We get my luggage checked in and myself checked in. We still have time before I have to go through security, and I have to leave my dog and my dad behind for God only knows how long. I'm overwhelmed by sadness. I don't want to leave my dad and Eleanor behind. I want them to come with me. I'm also scared; I haven't seen my mom in over a year. We have just started talking again on a regular basis since she found out I was flying down to live with her, which was only about two and an half weeks ago. She has no idea how out of control I am with opiates.

Since my father and I don't have a hugging relationship, I spend these last few minutes saying good-bye to Eleanor. My dad and I talk about how I am going to behave in Hawaii. He says to listen to my mom but still call my dad if she is doing anything she shouldn't be doing ... like having men over while I'm there. Then he tells me how exciting this will be for me—to live in Hawaii and to get back on methadone.

Neither of us mentions that I am running away from Wisconsin because I'm wanted by the police, although I do worry about getting on the plane. I worry about getting on all three of my planes. I'm afraid the police are going to read my name on the flight register and come arrest me. I don't know that the world is so big and full of criminals that nobody really cares that I ran away from rehab and am wanted for running out on my probation agent.

Time rushes by too fast, and soon it's time for me to go through security check. It's time for me to say my good-byes to my dad and my beloved dog Eleanor. I don't want to start crying. If I do it will make it harder for my dad to say good-bye. He'll worry even more, and we don't need that.

I turn to my dad, holding Eleanor in my arms tightly. I tell him, "She has to sleep in the bed with you during naps and at night, and she needs lots of attention."

My dad says, "Don't worry, Anna, she is my little princess. She has two other big dogs who she loves to play with (Shawnee and Shasta), but Eleanor will get all the attention she needs."

I say, "Thank you, Dad. I wish you and Eleanor were coming with me."

My dad promises that he will get all of Eleanor's paper work in order for her to come down to Hawaii so she can live with me. She just has to do a 120-day quarantine thing to make sure she doesn't have rabies. He promises that he too will fly down for Christmas with Eleanor to visit.

I tell my dad for the last time that I love him, and I tell Eleanor that I love her and give her a million little kisses one last time. Then I quickly turn around and go through the security checkpoint. I look back and wave good-bye to my dad and Eleanor as I take off my shoes. That is the last I see of them.

I don't start crying until I'm on the plane and the realization sets in that I am not going to see either of them for an unknown amount of time. I'm leaving my dad all alone in the middle of nowhere, in a big cabin meant for a family. I'm going down to Hawaii to be with his wife, whom he is now separated from, not legally, but mentally. He's taking a big chance on me, his heroin-addicted daughter, going down to Hawaii where her mother is living out her fantasy life, a drunken floozy.

When my dad gets home he's going to find syringes up in the loft that was my bedroom. I'm scared that my dad is going to commit suicide. I think about killing myself a lot still. I know that my dad is suicidal. He once told me that if it wasn't for me he would kill himself. He told me that right after my sister died in 2003. I know that I just don't want to live anymore, especially if I have to live without heroin. I know my drug use is killing my father and mother, but she's found a way to cover it up. I know I'm a selfish little brat. I hate myself and want to die. I hate who I've become; I hate who I always have been. I know it would be horrible for my parents at first, but if they just push through a couple of years, they will find that they are better off without me.

My mind is spinning: suicide, dope, suicide, dope, and on and on. I dig into my purse and take out five methadone 10 mgs, and five Valium 5 mgs. I take a drink of the vodka and orange juice I ordered when I boarded the plane. After I take the pills I sit back and relax and wait for the plane to cross the Midwest and land in Phoenix.

By the time we start to prepare for landing I'm out of my mind high. At some point I must have taken a Snickers out of my purse to eat and nodded out in the middle of the first bite, so the flight attendant asks me if I am okay.

I say, "Yes. Why?"

She says, "You should go look at yourself in the mirror before we have to buckle in for landing."

So I get up and go to the lavatory and look in the mirror, and my face is covered with melted chocolate from the Snickers bar. It's all over my face. Now I understand why the family sitting next to me wouldn't let their baby near me. When I'm loaded I often mumble to myself, move my arms sporadically, and have a hard time keeping myself conscious as I'm nodding in and out. I must have seemed like a crazy person to the family next to me. I just laugh to myself. I wipe the chocolate of my face, unfazed because I feel too good. I go back to my seat, and it's time to buckle in for the descent into the Phoenix airport.

We deboard at Phoenix, Arizona. I have nine hours to find my gate, get something to eat, go to the bathroom, and sober up enough to watch my purse through the night. As soon as I get off the plane I notice I have swollen up. This has happened before, right after my suicide attempt. It means that I have put too much stress on my kidneys. My ankles are gigantic, and so are my hands and stomach.

First thing I need is a wheelchair so I can elevate my legs to bring the swelling down, plus I can nod out and not seem so odd. So I go and get a wheelchair. Even though this airport is huge, there is a wheelchair at every corner, it seems.

After finding my wheelchair I go outside and smoke a cigarette. I imagine Hawaii and my life there. I'm twenty-five now, and this will be the furthest from Wisconsin I have ever lived. Getting over being without Eleanor is proving itself easier than I had predicted. I have too much on my mind—death, drugs, moving. On my way back in through security I am pulled aside and my stuff is looked through thoroughly. Thank goodness all my pills are in my name.

After my smoke, I go to the bathroom. There is a full-length mirror in there. I stand up and look at myself. I am swollen to twice my size. Even my arms, belly, and face are huge. I try to pee, but I can't. I know it's a problem with kidneys. While in the bathroom, I change from winter clothes into summer clothes. I put on a long, flowing, pink patchwork skirt and a pink tank top. I pull my long curly hair into a ponytail. I put some powder on my face and mascara on my lashes. I get back in my wheelchair and wheel myself around the airport.

Before I know it, it's 10:00 pm and the crowds of people have cleared out. I'm still swollen and in my wheelchair. There are about five of us who have to wait until 5:00 am for our plane to take off. So we have six hours left until our plane leaves. We all huddle together, and we all take turns sleeping. I take only two methadone and one Valium, so I don't get too high. I get high just enough to feel great but not nod out.

It's my turn to sleep, and when 4:00 am rolls around someone wakes me up and I go and get a coffee. Then I go back to my gate and wait to board the plane. My next flight is a short flight, for AZ to LAX. From LAX I fly to Honolulu, Hawaii.

The rest of my flights are dull. From LA to Hawaii I watch the in-flight movie and nod out. When we go in for our descent I get really excited. This is it. I'm moving to Hawaii. I'm moving in with my mom. This could either be a good thing or a bad thing.

When I get off the plane I'm overwhelmed by the smells of Hawaii. The airport is open to the outside. It seems to have no roof or outside walls, just gates. Everywhere I look there are flowers, and their aroma is very fragrant. I can smell the sea too, and the salt in the air. Palm trees are everywhere. I feel the midday sun's rays beating down on my bare shoulders. There is so much to take in, but I have to find the baggage claim and my mom and call my dad and tell him I'm safe and sound. My high has worn off, and I feel agitated, but I feel that I should see my mother for the first time in a year sober.

My cell phone rings, and I answer. It's Pete. I haven't spoken to him in a while. I called him right after I got out of the hospital to tell him I was moving to Hawaii. I stop what I'm doing and sit down in the sun to speak with him. He says, "Anna, are you in Hawaii yet?"

I say, "I literally just got off the plane a few minutes ago and am looking for my luggage and my mom right now."

He asks what it's like so far, and I tell him the airport is huge and open.

Then Pete gets to why he called. He called to tell me that he cancelled my cell phone line. As of July 1 I won't have an active cell phone. It's mid-May, and it's really no big deal. What this really means is that Pete and I are truly breaking up. I don't think either of us really wants to break up; our lives have just taken us on two very separate paths. As far as the cell phone goes, my mom can always get me a new one in July. Pete and I say our good-byes and our last I love yous.

I stand up and go look for my mom. She's probably the my baggage claim by now. I walk back toward baggage claim and walk in one big circle until I finally see my mom. She is with a man. He's about fifty, five foot eleven, with a medium build and gray hair that is long and kept in a ponytail with a nondescript baseball hat on top. He is wearing typical tropic clothes: khaki shorts, a Budweiser T-shirt, and sandals. He is handsome for a fifty-year-old man. He's definitely not as handsome as my dad is, though.

My mom looks really good. She has lost a lot of weight in the past year. Here I am swollen twice the size I really am, jetlagged and hungry. When my mom hugs me she puts a lei on me. She introduces the man next to her as Scott, her friend and our apartment manager. In my mind he's the reason my dad is home alone with a broken heart right now. Little did I know it at the time.

We walk out of the airport, and my image of Hawaii as a peaceful, laid-back island full of huts and tiki shacks along with mansions on the ocean is shattered. What I see is skyscrapers as far as my eyes can see and the highway in front of me, on which we are doing ninety mph in a little old Ford Topaz. The mountains are to the left of me, the ocean to the right. Up the mountains halfway are houses packed in like sardines. They aren't the nice manicured houses I had imagined but are broken-down rickety shacks. The roads up the mountains are winding and narrow. To the right on the ocean front it's mostly hotels that reach to the sky seemingly touching the sun. There are lots of sales stands selling trinkets for tourists. The closer we get to Waikiki Beach the more sales stands there are.

Our apartment is in Waikiki Beach, and as we approach I can smell the salt in the air get more and more pungent. The ocean is close by. I notice that Caucasians are in the minority; the majority here is Asian. I sit quietly in the back seat and watch as everything passes me by. My mom speaks to Scott about her plans for the next three days, which she has off work. Most of her plans include showing me around the area, getting me acquainted with the bus system, and finding the methadone clinic.

We arrive at our apartment. There are four floors, and we are on the first floor. The outside of the apartment complex is nothing special. It's surrounded by other buildings. On one side is an Internet shop, and on the other side is a scuba-diving store. At the front of the complex is a big gate where cars go in and out, and there is a door that is locked. My mom and I get keys.

Scott gets out and goes to his apartment. My mom thanks him for the ride, and I thank him also. Now it's just me all swollen and my mom, two people who have to get to know each other again. Their love for one another is still there. I can tell that my mom is excited that I'm there. I'm excited to be there. Then I walk in the door.

The apartment is tiny, and she pays $1,200 a month. There is a tiny living room with a really small kitchen right off of it. Then there is the bedroom—the one bedroom with two twin beds. My mom and I are going to be getting really close; we are going to be like sisters. We are sharing a room. It's not cheap to live in Waikiki Beach, Hawaii. The bathroom is just as tiny as you'd expect from the rest of the house. There's just enough room to turn around in. Then there is this little room in the middle of the apartment like in a hotel room that has a mirror and a counter where you can put your makeup on, do your hair, etc. To ease this shock I dig into my purse and take three methadone pills and two Valium.

Before the medication kicks in my mom shows me the small space she set aside for my stuff. Luckily I packed lightly. I unpack, and as soon as I'm done my mom has the couch ready for me to put my legs up to get the swelling in them down. It's getting painful for me to stand when I'm not high. My mom is worried that my kidneys are failing and wants to take over the duty of handing out my methadone and Valium to me. She has no idea how addicted I am to this medication, and I tell her no. I have a routine. I make the excuse that I'll soon be on the methadone from the clinic anyway. She thinks I'm on methadone for pain, when in reality I get methadone because I lied to the doctor and said I had full-blown AIDS.

While I'm lying down with my feet up in the air, my mom walks over to the grocery store and gets us both a piece of chocolate cake from the bakery. By the time she gets back I'm loaded. My speech is slurred, I'm nodding out, and she just thinks I'm very tired from all the traveling. I end up nodding out face first in the chocolate cake. I wake up with chocolate cake all over my face. So far Hawaii has found my face filled with chocolate twice on nods. If I didn't have methadone in me, I would miss Eleanor and my dad so much that I would be crying in the bathroom. My mom would feel bad for me. I think it's better this way. I still miss Eleanor and my dad, but I can dull all my emotions with pain pills and Valium. Hopefully I can use some black tar heroin here in Hawaii. Back in Wisconsin I've only used China white heroin. I just have to keep my methadone dose low so I can feel the heroin when I shoot it up. Plus I have the beach to look forward to. I nod out over and over until I finally fall asleep for the night on the couch with my feet up. My first night in Hawaii has gone pretty well aside from the chocolate-cake face.

The next morning I wake up and the swelling is almost all gone. My mom has a big day planned for us. She wants to show me all of Honolulu. She always plans big, and we end up doing one thing and being too tired to do anything else the rest of the day. I just want to find Chinatown, where the dope is being sold, and I'm good. What number bus do I take to get there and what number bus to I take to get back? I'm sure once I start out at the methadone clinic all I have to do is ask someone there who I need to know to buy the heroin and show that person my methadone bottles and track marks. Hopefully that will do it.

The number 19 bus takes us to the DASH Methadone Clinic, and it goes straight through downtown Chinatown. We catch the number 19 bus, and it's very crowded. It's early in the morning, 8:00 am, and workers and school kids alike are trying to get to their respective places of business. There is nowhere to sit, so it's ass to glass for us standing passengers.

The ride there is about an half hour. This will be my morning trip every day from now on, into the foreseeable future. The clinic opens at 5:30 am and closes at 11:30 am.

We reach our stop, and the clinic is in a strip mall with three levels. The DASH Methadone Clinic is on the third level. We walk through a parking garage to get to that elevator. Once off the elevator I notice the smell—it smells just like jail. They must use the same cleaners. We walk down a hallway following the signs and get to a waiting room. I get to the window and announce my presence.

The lady at the front desk is a robust Samoan woman with long, thick, black hair and a dark complexion. She is wearing three gold bracelets on her left arm. I've noticed a lot of the native Hawaiians and local Pacific Islanders wear these bracelets.

The lady at the desk asks me my name and then tells me to have a seat and wait for the nurse. So I sit next to my mom. I feel close to my mom again, as if there was no year that passed with little communication and lots of animosity. The mother-daughter relationship is stronger than I had expected.

My mother and I are talking about my swelling when the nurse calls my name. My mom stays behind and waits in the waiting room even though I invite her in with me.

The first thing the nurse does is have me pee in a cup. The she asks me how I used heroin—did I smoke, inject, snort, or take pills. I tell I was an IV heroin user. She asks to see my track marks. I show her, and she becomes really reassuring. She takes my blood pressure, pulse, and respirations. I'm in mild withdrawal and have an empty bottle of methadone and Valium with me. The nurse is small white lady who is all over the place but is kind-hearted. She keeps reassuring me that I will get dosed today. I explain to her that I just flew into Hawaii hours ago from Wisconsin and I don't have insurance. I'm worried because my mom doesn't have the money it costs for me to dose at the clinic in Green

Bay, Wisconsin. It's cheaper to dose here in Hawaii, but it will still be a strain on my mom's pocketbook. The nurse hands me an emergency medical form, which gives me emergency insurance so my methadone will be paid for by the insurance company.

Knowing that I'll get dosed today and that it's free makes me feel much better. I'm not going to be as big a drain on my mom financially as I had thought.

While waiting in the back to dose I meet another patient waiting to meet with his counselor. I quietly ask him where to find heroin. He leans in and says, "Go to the Fort St. Mall between 6:00 am and 8:00 am in Chinatown. Look for a guy with a T-shirt wrapped around his head. His name is Uncle Q. You know to get high on H while on methadone you have to stay below 50 mgs."

I ask, "Is this junkie-to-junkie or are you running me around in circles?"

He says, "Junkie-to junkie. My name is Uncle Knuckles."

I tell him my name and that I just moved here. I thank him for his advice. Uncle Knuckles gets called into his counselor's office, and I get called into my new counselor's office where I have tons of paper work to fill out. By the time I'm finished the doctor has called back and I can officially dose. I go up to the dosing window and drink the juice. In Green Bay the juice was pink and tasted sweet. Here it's clear and tastes like chewed aspirin. They start me out at 30 mgs. I can't go up much more, if any at all, if I want to get high off junk.

On my first outing to the clinic alone I'm new to town, and my first bus ride alone to the methadone clinic is stressful. I'm not quite sure which stop I should ring the bell at, but I know it's when Best Buy is in sight, so I make it.

I wake up in the morning at 6:00 am thinking tha this will leave me time to get to Chinatown's Fort St. Mall and meet up with Uncle Q, hoping Knuckles will be there to introduce me and give me Uncle Q's number so I can call to score instead of having to score on the street more than necessary. Unfortunately I didn't get on the bus this morning until 7:30 am and don't get to the clinic until almost 8:30 am.

When I make my way to the waiting room of the clinic I see a batch of the clients. When I walk in all the men in the waiting room lift their heads and take notice of me. I seem to attract junkies with my sundress and bikini underneath, long, flowing, dark, curly hair, blue eyes with smoky eyeliner, pale skin, and flip-flops. My face is soft and my nose perfectly straight and just the right size for my face. My lips are small and light colored, making my eyes pop. Walking down the street people stop me about once a week and tell me how beautiful my eyes are.

I sit down next to the one guy I think is attractive. I can tell he is homeless; almost all of the people in the waiting room are homeless. I can smell all different kinds of body odor from all different kinds of people. The one guy I think is attractive seems to take no notice of me. He's too out of it. He's on the nod already; what he needs methadone today for I don't know. Normally when junkie men who are not too high see me, they see my track marks and bruises and offer to get high with me. Since we are on heroin, and heroin takes away from the libido, sex takes a distant second to getting high. Most junkies just want someone pretty with them, someone they can just think about having sex with while they are high. Once in a while, if the dope isn't very strong and I am attracted to the guy, I will have sex with him, but it's an emotionless sex. It's more like masturbation, but with another human being.

The guy on the other side of the attractive guy is a punk. He has a long blonde Mohawk that isn't spiked. He's got red hair on the sides where it's shaved. His body is tall and lanky with a bit of a hunchback. He is covered in freckles and faded tattoos. You can tell that his fair skin isn't made for the Hawaiian sun. His face is narrow, and his eyes are small and lizard-like. His mouth is missing most of its teeth, and what teeth are left are brown and pointy. It seems he can't keep his mouth shut. I hear him talking to everybody who comes in the waiting area. His nervous habit is playing with his unspiked Mohawk hair. When he does close his mouth, I can feel his lizard-like eyes stare a hole through me.

I feel a tap on my shoulder, and with reservation I look over my left shoulder and see his wide-open toothless smile gleaming back at me. He asks me my name, and I tell him Anna. He says, "Hi Anna. I'm Kevin. You must be new here, because I come at all different times and I've never seen you here before."

I say, "Yes, I am new here. I just moved here from Wisconsin."

He asks how I got hooked on heroin. I tell him that when I was around nineteen my dad had a prescription for Percocet. Then he got Oxycontin and then morphine. Then I met a dealer who was dealing Dilaudid and heroin. So it just sort of fell into my lap. Plus I always wanted to use, since I was in seventh grade and found out that Kurt Cobain and Courtney Love were heroin addicts. I just wanted that sort of lifestyle. I wanted to be numb. I knew what pain pills felt like because I had gotten my appendix out when I was ten, and I pushed that pain button every few seconds.

He asks how old I am, and I tell him twenty-four. I ask him how old he is; he tells me forty-one. I didn't bother to ask how he got hooked; that would be a long story. He asks what kind of music I listen to, and I tell him I like punk, underground, garage rock, and stoner rock. As for bands, obviously I love Nirvana, Hole, Melvins, Pixies, Leadbelly, Butthole Surfers, Eagles of Death Metal, Queens of the Stone Age, and the list could go on and on.

"How about yourself?"

He asks me if I've ever heard of D something.

I say, "No."

He tells me they are a punk band from California and that he used to be a guitar player in this band. They used to be a pretty famous punk band, as famous as punk bands get. Pretty underground. I was never into California underground punk; I'm more of a Washington, Oregon, underground listener. I ask why he's not in the band anymore.

He says, "Because I got strung out. I moved to Hawaii because it was easier to be homeless here."

Then he drops what he's been waiting to ask, "Do you want to hang out after dosing? We could score some dope or pills and go to the dollar movies to get out of the heat. My friend will be coming along. This is what we do every day."

I don't really want to hang out with this guy, but if he has a connection and I can meet this connection, then I will have a connection. All on my first outing by my lonesome. If I say yes, he may think I like him sexually, which I do not. As long as he brings a friend, then it's not like a date. I check my cell phone as if I have a text message from someone, and I tell him to meet me downstairs behind the parking garage when he's done dosing.

I take my dose and wait for Kevin outside. I am smoking a cigarette when he gets down to me. Of course when he sees that I have real cigarettes he asks to bum one. Damn homeless. We start to walk down the parking lot driveway, and we walk about a quarter mile to a different bus stop. Kevin asks what part of Honolulu I live in. I tell him Waikiki Beach, and he tells me that this bus stop is better to take home. Almost all these buses go to Waikiki, and all of them go to Chinatown. This was a good thing to learn, because if I had taken the bus I took to get to the methadone clinic back home, I would have to sit and wait for it to come back around for thirty minutes. At this bus stop I will only wait ten minutes at most. I'm learning that the buses here are fast.

Kevin and I take the first bus that pulls up to the stop. It's 10:00 am, and there is nobody on the bus except for some elderly Asian women up front. Kevin goes straight to the back of the bus, and I follow. We want to talk about drugs, and we don't want to let everyone know we are users, although Kevin could be spotted for a user ten miles away. While on the short bus ride to Chinatown we talk about what we want to buy. I want a gram of heroin. That's all I have money for. If it's pills I prefer Dilaudid, but Kevin doesn't know how much they go for because he gets morphine. He's sure Dilaudid is more than morphine. If we can't get either of these things, we buy Xanax. We can always surely get Xanax bars. "Crack heads," he tells me, "are always giving up their Xanax and Valium scrips to feed their daily crack addiction." Mix methadone and Xanax and you get a feeling close to being high on H. Not the rush, just the nodding out.

I'm surprised when we get off at Fort St. Mall. I was told that there weren't any dealers out after 8:00 am. Plus Kevin is so conspicuous as a drug user, and there's all the police presence around the mall. I just thought he would go where the crack heads go. I'm willing to bet that Kevin smokes either crack or ice or both, because junkies don't look so eaten up. Junkies tend to look like death with breath, with skin and bones bags under their eyes, younger than their years. Crack and ice heads look like they're being eaten up by their drugs, with tooth and bone loss in their faces, zits, and sores on their faces and all over their bodies; they look older than their years.

Kevin asks for thirty-five cents to use the pay phone. He takes my order, my back-up order, and my back-up-back-up order. Suddenly there is another man standing next to Kevin at the pay phones. This guy is just a heroin junkie, I can tell. He's about thirty-five with a beard and long, light brown hair, He has thick eyebrows and is thin with a dirty T-shirt and a pair of holey jeans.

One junkie can spot another junkie just by the feeling they give off. It's a strange ability. I believe it's like the feeling victims have just before being struck by lightning. They say they feel a buzz and see a bluish light. It's very subtle, but it's there. As with junkies, we can spot each other in a crowd instantly, like we are going to be struck by lightning. That's the feeling I get when I see the man lean against the pay phone that Kevin is using.

Kevin talks on the phone for close to five minutes. When he gets done he talks to his friend before coming over to where I'm sitting and introduces me to his friend Mike. Mike is attractive, with big blue eyes and brown hair that is lightened by the sun. His skin is tanned by the sun, and all this makes his eyes more attractive—piercing, like he see right through me. It almost scares me.

Kevin tells me as he sits down in the chair next to me, with Mike in the chair across from mine, outside a Korean restaurant in this outdoor mall/collage campus, that his man is going to meet him a few streets down at a smoothie shop in fifteen minutes. He says I should sit tight here with Mike and he will be back in twenty minutes.

I think to myself, *Fuck, I'm not going to meet a connection today. I just sent some guy I just met off with forty dollars, and he might not come back.* To think just a half hour ago things seemed so promising.

I've never trusted middle men. They always rip you off somehow. Some just take your money and run; some come back with half the amount of dope you ordered but all the money gone in their pockets.

At least he left his friend Mike behind. Mike and I converse about drugs. I ask him how long he's been using. He tells me nearly fifteen years. I ask, "Are you sick right now?"

He says, "A little. A runny nose, watery eyes, body aches. Nothing a shot of H won't fix."

Then I ask him where he's from. He tells me he's from San Diego. He moved here for a job loading ships. He still has that job, amazingly. He works second shift. He spends his days scoring and then using and then going to the dollar movies or panhandling for extra money. He rents a small room off the sidewalk that only fits a bed. That's where we'll be going to fix if Kevin comes back with the drugs. Mike senses that I think Kevin is going to rip me off, and he reassures me that Kevin hasn't steered him wrong in the two and a half years he's known him.

I ask Mike, "Do you know the person he scores from?"

Mike says, "Yes. He's the same guy I get my gear from. His gear is good. It's not all cut to shit like the stuff Uncle Q sells out here in the morning. Anyway, Uncle Q's days are numbered selling out in the open the way he does. You should prove yourself and see if our guy will take you on as a new customer. Are you a regular, daily user?"

I reply, "Yes."

He says, "That's the only kind of customers he takes on. You have a regular supply of cash?" he asks.

"Yes," I tell him. I think to myself that my mom does at least.

I see Kevin round the corner, and my heart rate accelerates. He's got a sort of skip to his step, which I assume means he got what he went for. He sees me watching him, and Mike watching too, and he smiles with those few brown pointy teeth. It seems like forever for him to get to us, but finally he takes the seat next to me, leans in, and says, "Mike, can we use your place?" Mike nods.

"First we have to stop at Longs drugstore and pick up a bottle of water and an extra spoon along with a few syringes," says

Kevin. I know this is for me, and I just spent all my money on the heroin. This means that I have to steal a spoon and a bottle of water. We all need needles, so whoever has money will go to the pharmacy and buy the fits. No way can we could steal fits without robbing the entire pharmacy.

I walk into Longs. It's an old drugstore with no cameras, just those blind spot mirrors. I go straight to the measuring spoons first. I have a hard time finding a metal measuring spoon. They all seem to be plastic. Finally after I give up looking I see an ice cream scooper small enough to cook up a shot in. I put it in my purse quickly. Then I walk over to the coolers and pull out a bottle of water. It only costs seventy-five cents. I can afford that, so I go to the checkout and buy it.

We get out of Longs without any trouble. Now we have to walk four blocks in the blistering sun to Mike's room. On the walk I call my mom and tell her I'm in Chinatown looking around and people watching at the college campus at Fort St. Mall and I'll be home this afternoon. It's already noon, and the sun is high in the sky. Sweat is beading up on my forehead and on my upper lip, my back, under my breasts, and on the back of my neck under all my hair. I wish I had a hair tie.

We get to Mike's room; it's as big as a small walk-in closet. It has a concrete floor with a twin-size mattress on it. There are some shelves hanging up and a plastic bin with some clothes in it. On top of the bin is like a night stand, with a small lamp and Mike's bag of works, which he keeps in a women's makeup bag with a zipper. He keeps it in there mainly because of the zipper. Cops can't search anything with a zipper without a search warrant. The place is a mess. He has cookers from the needle exchange lying around, but they are all used. So are all the tubes of sterile water. All he has left from the exchange are clean cottons.

Kevin pulls out the tiny ziplock baggies with superman logos on them. Inside the bag is what looks like black gum that is oily. He hands me my 0.2 g of black tar heroin. I want to start out slowly. I've never felt black tar before. It's sticky, but it smells the same. Vinegary.

I watch Mike cook up his shot to see if you cook up black tar any differently. You don't. So I put my piece in the ice cream scooper and take my fit and fill it with 80 cc of water. I squirt it into the spoon. I grab a lighter off the plastic bin and put it under the spoon until the water boils and the black tar is melted into a liquid. When it is I drop in the cotton and take the spike, put it in the cotton, and pull back on the plunger, sucking up the heroin. It's so dark I wonder how I will see my blood blossom in when I hit a vein. Kevin gives me one of Mike's belts to tie off with. I put it around my upper arm and pump my fist and smack the inside of my elbow until a vein shows itself. It's been a while since I shot up, so my vein shows itself a lot faster than usual. Normally I have to poke and prod around for a half hour to an hour just to find a vein.

When the vein pops out I slide the spike in and pull back on the plunger; the fit fills with blood. I push the plunger in slowly. I let go of the belt I was holding with my teeth. I pull the spike out of my arm, and blood drips down my arm. I quickly lick it up and keep my mouth over the hole for a few seconds until it stops bleeding.

I'm used to the smack hitting me within ten seconds of pulling the spike out. It's a warm rush running up your back as all feelings disappear and euphoria sets in.

Nothing like that is happening. I either didn't do enough or I got ripped off. I'm angry, but slowly a warm sensation crawls up my back and my head gets heavy. Slowly all the world's pain and fears disappear. I barely notice as Kevin falls out on the nod with a cigarette in his hand. He took a big shot. Mike and I both light a smoke, but neither of us speak a word. We sit silently for a good ten minutes.

I'm the first one to break the silence. My speech is slurred. Kevin is still in and out of it. I say to Mike, "This stuff comes on a lot slower than the heroin at home."

He says, "Yeah, black tah Heroin is all I have ever tried, but I have tried Dilaudid and Oxycontin and morphine. Those ahll hit you almost instantly. Ah-most bh-fore the needle's out."

I think I caught everything he said, but I can't be sure. He is slurring his speech pretty badly.

It's extraordinarily hot in his little room. If he had a fan it might be bearable, but I have to get out of there. Kevin was in no shape to walk. Mike and I both talk about tearing off a piece of his heroin for ourselves, but I decide against it. He did me a favor today, and I didn't want any bad karma. Mike and I start to walk to the bus stop to get to the dollar theater. When I get to the bus stop I realize that I only have enough money for bus fare home. So we decide to go back to Fort St. Mall and sit in the shade right outside the door of an air-conditioned restaurant.

Both Mike and I are chatty. Now that we are high we want to talk about anything and everything. We find a good place to sit, and then people Mike knows start coming up to him and saying hello and meeting me. Some ask if I'm Mike's new girlfriend. I meet a lot of people I saw at the methadone clinic that morning and even more junkies not from the methadone clinic. Almost everyone asked to bum a smoke. Mike tells me never to pull out a pack of cigarettes around here, always go into your purse and pull out one at a time. If someone asks for one, say it was your last one. Otherwise if you bum one cigarette they will never stop asking you.

We sit there for about an hour and an half. Kevin comes stumbling over asking why we left him and talking about how he was perfectly fine. There's no use arguing with him, so we just apologize.

The time comes for me to go back to Waikiki, and I thank both Kevin and Mike several times. I take Kevin's number. Then I catch the number 13 bus back to my mom's apartment. When I get there she is baking an apple pie. She asks what I thought of Chinatown. I tell her about all the homeless and panhandlers. I say it was like Central Park in a lot of ways, just more Asians and college kids in a smaller park. My mom tells me that she is going to the bar tonight to play darts and I'm welcome to come along. I tell her I don't know what I am going to do. It depends what was on TV. I ended up staying home and getting high.

Chapter 5

After living in Hawaii for a while and using heroin every day on top of my daily dose of methadone, I end up strung out again.

It's a warm sunny day at the Fort St. Mall. The mall is abuzz with students and homeless alike. I'm sitting around in the grassy knoll trying to read *Wild Boys* by William S. Burroughs. I can't get through a page without falling over and nodding out. I have shot up and eaten 6 mg Xanax bars. I am nearly ODing.

In my own drugged-out world, I don't notice three men surround me on the grass. I wake up a little when one of the guys takes the book out of my hand. I tried to focus on him and notice an Asian-looking face with freckles and rotten front teeth. He's smiling at me and says, "You're calling a lot of attention to yourself over here, and the cops are all around today."

I try my hardest not to slur my words as I speak. I say back to this guy, "Thanks for the info. I'll catch a bus home."

This guy cuts me off and says, "You'll never make it home alone. You're too out of it. Let me take you home."

I say okay and tell him we need to catch the number 19 bus; it stops right in front of my apartment. So this guy I don't know helps me up off the ground, picks up my bags, and supports my weight on his arm as I drag my feet trying to keep up.

He tells me his name is Charlie Jenkins. When we get off the bus I ask if he wants to meet my mom. He says sure. So I get to the apartment building and my mom and landlord along with a few of their bar friends are sitting outside drinking beer. I bring Charlie over to their little gathering to meet my mom.

The next part I don't remember as the Xanax wiped out my memory. From what my mom tells me she could tell I was using, and she asks me what I remember about that night. I do remember waking up standing in front of the light switch with my hand in the air like I was going to switch it on or off. My mom says, "Yes, that happened. I woke you up to turn out the lights and it took you a half hour."

The next morning I wake up needing my dose of methadone and my shot of heroin. I have to catch the bus across town to the clinic. I'm up early, so I sit and smoke. My mom gets up a few minutes after me. We both look like hell. My mom asks if I'm going to see my new boyfriend today. I look at her perplexed. I don't have a boyfriend. She says, "That's not what you said yesterday. You told me Charlie was your boyfriend, and you even kissed him on the lips and gave him your phone number and told him to call as soon as he woke up." I think to myself, *Yuck, he had bad teeth.* Mom tells me he only left when she had to tell him it was time to go and that she would watch over me.

On the bus ride over to the clinic, I try to remember this Charlie. Then it comes to me: there were three guys who were worried that I was attracting too much attention from the police. I'm lucky those three guys didn't steal anything or gang rape and murder me. I have to more careful about how many Xanax bars I take. Luck was just on my side yesterday.

I had put on my white swimsuit and a mini sweat skirt with flip-flops to go and pick up my drugs for the day. I didn't even brush my teeth this morning. I'm just lazy. Anyway, I plan on going straight home from scoring. My mom will be at work tonight. My phone rings when I'm about six stops away from the methadone clinic.

"Hello."

"Hi, Anna. It's Charlie from yesterday."

"Oh yes, I remember you." *A little*, I think to myself.

Charlie asks, "Did you really mean what you said last night, that I was your boyfriend?"

I almost gasp. Who the hell thinks a drugged-out girl means a word she says? I stutter a bit in answering the question posed. "I don't really know you, Charlie, but I do appreciate you helping me out yesterday, keeping me away from the cops and all. But I was high off my ass when I said those things."

Even though I don't want to I tell Charlie that I'm on my way downtown on the bus and will probably stop at the mall for a fruit drink on my way home. "If you want to meet up and let me buy you a fruit drink to thank you, I'll meet you by the church in an half hour," I tell him. I pick a shady spot in the mall but a place where the security guards can see what's going on.

Before I meet up with Charlie, I have to meet up with Kevin, who has now become my dealer. He lives in a tent city just outside of Chinatown, down by the river. There are a lot of homeless down there. That's where I stop every morning to get my heroin. I buy my day's worth of heroin and put it in my vagina just in case. From tent city I walk seven blocks to the Fort St. Mall where I said I'd meet Charlie.

When I get to the bench in front of the church, I see Charlie and two other men. I'm attracted to one guy in particular. He's blonde, young, dirty, and skinny, with big blue eyes. I can tell immediately that all three are dope fiends. Next to the attractive guy is an older man in his late fifties or early sixties. He's got long black and grey hair and messed-up teeth. He is Polynesian. Charlie is dressed in his Sunday best. He's half white and half Asian. He is wearing those hip square glasses that tint themselves in the sunlight.

There is a fire hydrant next to the bench in front of it a little, and it's shaped like a T, so it's big enough to sit on. I take a seat, and Charlie greets me eagerly. It's just about 9:00 am, and the sun isn't high in the sky so the air isn't hot. It's still a little cool from the night—my favorite time of day in Hawaii. Charlie holds out his hand and tries to grab my hand to hold it, but I put my hands in my purse to get a cigarette. Charlie's face shows his disappointment. I wasn't too subtle.

I start up a conversation with the blonde guy. He tells me his name is Alex. We talk about my close call with the police yesterday. He tells me that the policeman was walking up to me when they surrounded me. They told the policeman that I was really hung over and they were going to bring me home. As Alex and I talk, Charlie and the older man talk amongst themselves.

I'm hitting it off with Alex, and I make a little small talk with Charlie and the older guy, who introduces himself as Sam. The sun starts to get high in the sky, so I ask Alex for his phone number before I leave. He tells me that he doesn't have a phone but that he's always with Charlie, so I should just call Charlie's phone if I want to talk to him. Charlie walks away for a few seconds, and just as I'm walking out of the mall, he comes up to me and goes to shake my hand and drops two pills in it. I say, "See you later, Charlie, and thanks." I light a cigarette as I wait for the bus and look in my hand at the pills he gave me. They are two 2 mg Xanax bars.

When I get home, the first thing I do is get the heroin out from my crotch. I get my works out and cook up a shot. I hold off on the Xanax, not wanting what happened yesterday to happen today. After I take my shot, I jump in the shower and wash the blood off my hands and arms. I clean myself up. I get out of the shower, get dressed, brush my teeth, and smoke. I decide to call Alex. Of course when I call it's Charlie who answers and keeps me on the line with him for a good half hour if not more. He keeps telling what a sweet guy he is and how he always gets his heart broken. If only he could find someone like me, someone with the same addiction. I ask him how old he is, and he won't tell me at first. I prod a little, and he tells me he's thirty-two. I'll be twenty-five a few weeks from now on February 2. I've never liked anyone that much older than me. Charlie keeps on talking. I'm not even listening. In between breaths I ask to talk to Alex. He says "Sure, here he is."

"Hello Alex, it's Anna from yesterday and this morning." He laughs and tells me he gathered as much from listening to Charlie on the phone next to him. He tells me Charlie hasn't gone ten minutes without bringing me up since last night. I say, "Oh great," exasperated.

I ask Alex if he would like to come over and watch a movie, eat, and sit in air conditioning with me. He accepts my invitation. I set out some food and go down to the grocery store and pick up some sweets. All heroin addicts have bad sweet tooths. After a while passes I hear the buzzer while lying in the bedroom next to the air conditioner. I run out to the door outside in the front, and to my utter disbelief I find Charlie standing there. I look at him, confused, and ask where is Alex. He says, "Oh he didn't have enough money to get a bus ride over here."

I don't want to bring Charlie into the apartment, so I tell him to stay there for a minutes and I run in and grab my purse. Then I come out from behind the locked outside door, and Charlie and I walk the few steps it takes to get to Starbucks. Charlie doesn't stop talking. I can't believe that instead of giving Alex the dollar fifty for bus fare, he decided to come over instead.

I order an iced cappuccino, and Charlie gets a regular coffee. When Charlie finally lets me get a word in edgewise I tell him I'm not interested in him, although I wouldn't mind being friends. I say that out of pity. I tell him I'm attracted to Alex. Charlie then goes off on a rant about how horrible Alex is. He says, "He's homeless and sleeping on his floor, always eating my food, and then he tells me he's only nineteen."

I'm a bit thrown by how young Alex is. I'm six years older than he is. There goes my feeling for Alex. I don't say this to Charlie, who then goes on to talk about himself nonstop. I end up cutting him off and telling him I'm going to go home. He thinks I invited him, and I have to tell him I'm going home alone. It seems the harder

I try to get away from him the tighter he hangs on. We finish our drinks, and Charlie invites me to his house tomorrow. He says he will surprise me with something. I tell him I will come over as a friend.

The rest of the day I spend in the bedroom under the air conditioner watching *America's Next Top Model*. I order Subway for supper. I fall asleep before the last episode of the marathon, so I don't know who wins *America's Next Top Model* that season.

The next day I repeat my routine: clinic, Kevin, mall. From the mall I call Charlie's phone and ask him how to get to his apartment. I can take the 13 or 2 bus into Makiki, get off in front of the Safeway grocery store, and walk two blocks up the sidewalk. His apartment building is white and only one story. He lives in number 228.

I find the place easy enough, and I get to number 228. Before I knock I listen through the door. I hear a female voice asking Charlie when he's going to call so and so and pick up some heroin. I knock, and Alex opens the door with a big smile. I get into the room, and it's as big as two and a half jail cells. He has a mattress on the cement floor and a table with a microwave on it and a bunch of noodles. His clothes are all over the place. I see a roach run across the room. There is barely enough room to fit all of us. All of us includes, me, Alex, Charlie, and Charlie's good friend Harmony. Harmony is pretty. She is eight months pregnant, with new track marks up and down her arms and hands. She pulls out a crack pipe out and puts a rock in it and smokes, not offering any to anybody else. Charlie takes me to show me the bathrooms, and he tells me that Harmony is a prostitute and a bad addict. I ask him why she doesn't get on methadone while she's knocked up. He says because she not only uses heroin but she's a crystal meth head and a crack head to boot. She got knocked up by a John she picked up one night hooking. Then Charlie says he has a surprise for me, and we go back to the apartment. Inside, Charlie calls someone and makes an order for a bunch of heroin.

In the apartment it's got to be one hundred degrees, and it smells like piss. Then I notice that Harmony pisses in jars and puts them on the end of the mattress so she doesn't have to walk to the bathroom. I tell Charlie I'm hot, and he turns on this little fan. It does nothing to cool anyone off. Charlie gathers Harmony's money and asks Alex if he has any money; Alex has none. He doesn't ask me. Charlie tells us he's going to go cop. I ask if I can walk with him. I'll wait far away from the deal. He says yes. We had waited almost four hours for the dealer to call back and tell him where to meet him. It is now dusk outside and is cooling off.

The drug deal goes on behind the 7-Eleven across the road from the bus stop where I got off. I go to the front of the gas station and go inside to cool off and buy something to drink. I decide to buy everyone something to drink. I also buy a pack of cigarettes for all of us to share. The three of them were all smoking Charlie's cigarettes. When I come out, I wait another five minutes, and when Charlie doesn't come to get me, I get paranoid that he was just going to leave me there. So I peek behind the store and see Charlie standing next to a red Ford truck. A woman is in the driver's seat, and an older man with an amputee arm is in the passenger seat. I watch unnoticed as the quick handshake passing the drugs to Charlie takes place. I quickly turn around and go to the front of the store and pretend like I have just been waiting. Charlie apologizes for the wait. I say, "No big deal. Isn't it a nice night out?" We walk back to Charlie's squat.

As soon as we walk in the door, Harmony is at Charlie's feet begging for her piece. Charlie says I didn't get different baggies, so I have to cut it up and put it on the scale before we can do anything. Harmony had bought a half gram, Charlie had bought a gram, and he had gotten me a half gram. Nothing for Alex, although we all tear off a small piece for him. Harmony gives him a small rock of crack. After he measures it all out, I tell him straight out, "I'm not having sex with you for this, so if that's your plan you can just keep it."

He laughs and says, "No, that wasn't even on my mind." He hands me my half gram in a rolled-up ball. I pull off a big chunk, and Charlie hands me a new cooker and new syringe and tiny cottons with water in a tube, all from the needle exchange van.

It takes Harmony over a half hour to find a vein. I find a vein in two tries, and Charlie finds his in one try; Alex finds his in one too. Soon all our eyes are droopy and our mouths agape, looking at the TV but not watching it. We all have cigarettes in our hands, and we all burn everything. I worry about a fire, with Harmony on the bed with all those blankets, nodding out with that cigarette.

I end up falling asleep. I'm on the roach-infested floor when I wake up. Harmony and Charlie are on the bed together head to toe. It's about 2:00 am, and I ready myself to go home. I look in my wallet for the buck fifty I need for the bus, and I notice twenty dollars missing. That's when I noticed that Alex is gone. I wake up Charlie and Harmony. Charlie is missing a hundred dollars, and Harmony is missing nothing as she keeps her money on her body at all times. It doesn't seem as though he touched the heroin at all.

Since I don't have any money, I decide to walk home in the night air. I think to myself, *I should have given Alex more of my heroin. I was too greedy.* I get home and strip to my underwear and lie down on the couch. I'm out of it in no time. I don't wake up until my mom comes home from work at 7:00 am. We sit and chitchat for a while, but my mom is really tired and wants to get to bed. She's off tomorrow so she can get up early this afternoon and go to the bar with Scott.

After my morning routine I go to the library, where it's cool and there is a private bathroom where I can fix up. I don't do a big shot, just enough to feel good, as if I have no worries. I go to the computers and log in to read some blogs that I like. I always wanted to start a blog, but we never got a computer after 1995.

I go outside of the library in the back garden where there is seating in the shade, and I call my dad. I can tell by his voice that he is depressed. He tells me that the cabin he and my mom built after my dad retired is going to be foreclosed on. He has no idea what he's going to do with everything in there. He doesn't have room for it in an apartment, plus the dogs. He can't bring three dogs—two big dogs—and two cats to a small apartment in the city. I ask why this is happening, and he tells me that my mom isn't sending any money home to pay for her part of the cabin. He just can't make the payments. He says he is going to sell everything worth anything and give the rest to Goodwill. I ask about Eleanor, and he says she will be down there in four months when her tests come back. Other than that she's doing really good. He pats her belly as we talk. I say good-bye to my dad and good night. It's only 1:00 here, but it's 6:00 pm there.

I get off the phone and think about whether I should call Charlie. I end up calling him, and we meet in turtle park in Chinatown. While high I've come to a realization: Charlie would do anything for me. Could I pretend to be his girlfriend? If I did he would get my dope for me from now on, and I wouldn't have to chance buying the dope and getting caught. Plus it would be cheaper; Kevin charges me for getting it from his dealer.

I decide I can do it. I can pretend as long as I tell him I need to take it really slow. Only pecks on the lips. From then on Charlie and I are always in Fort St. Mall. He buys me cigarettes when I don't have money, and he buys me food and heroin and will take me to the dollar movies. I take full advantage of Charlie.

With me around, Harmony stops coming around as often. She still sleeps there some nights, but I'm not there, and I don't give a shit. She hooks most of the night, so she shows up at Charlie's around dawn, sleeps till noon or one, and leaves. At first Harmony tries to befriend me. I can tell she's jealous because I took her place as Charlie's pretend girlfriend. Soon she becomes resentful of me and avoids me every chance she gets.

Since I know Harmony isn't given Charlie any sex, and I'm not either, I wonder if he ever gets any. As I said, the most I give him is a peck on the lips and a hug every now and then. One day we are sitting in the mall watching all the hot chick students, and I ask Charlie if he has ever been laid. He is embarrassed and tells me no, but he has gone to brothels and had sex with whores. I wonder if he still does that or not. Charlie and I start to spend all our days together, I keep his squat clean, or as clean as I can get it. I have him wash all the blankets and take out Harmony's piss bottles. Charlie introduces me to his mom, an old Vietnamese lady. She drives a Mercedes, so I know she's not poor and is where Charlie gets money for smokes and drugs from. Charlie's mom doesn't speak English very well and tells him one day to collect bottles and cans; no shame in that. I laugh and make Charlie say it like her over and over. Charlie's white side is from his dad, who drank himself to death. He was a Vietnam vet and got his mom pregnant in Vietnam with his older brother, and then they had him a few years later.

Charlie watches out for me. He introduces me to all the pill pushers, crack addicts, crystal meth addicts, and the crazy people. After a while I start to think of Charlie as a real friend. Then one day I tell him about my mom's new credit card with the 1-800 number still on top. Charlie decides it would be a good idea if I call that number and get the card activated and we use it to buy some heroin. We're both broke, and Charlie's mom said he was cut off. This was the tenth time since I've known him that she's said that. I end up stealing the card, and two days later my mom catches me. She forbids me to ever see Charlie again. There's nothing I can do. She keeps me in the house for four full days and nights. I got so dope-sick that finally she lets me go to the methadone clinic. I'm just lucky she didn't call the cops on me.

After that I start to buy my heroin from Kevin again. I still go to Fort St. Mall every day for about an half hour to visit people or buy Xanax. I knew all the old homeless guys in the mall and bum them smokes. Just like a dog getting a teat, the homeless pretend to be excited to see me to get their cigarette.

Not too soon after the whole Charlie thing goes down, I'm in the mall visiting the lady who sold me Xanax when the guy from the clinic—the guy I liked who was sitting next to Kevin but who didn't pay attention to me—pulls up on his ten-speed bike. He comes over to make a buy, and I introduce myself. I still sort of like him, and I could use a new friend.

I say, "Hello, my name is Anna. We go to the same clinic. I've seen you there a few times."

He says, "Oh yeah. I think I remember seeing you before. My name is Jake." He has a surfer accent. He says things like "dude, rad, bra(bro), tubular."

I ask Jake if he wants to get a frozen fruit drink. He says, "Sure, but let's go to this one I know where it's really cheap. It's about four blocks down."

I ask Jake if he still uses heroin, and he says, "For sure. I use coke, crack, ice, and weed too." Jake is somewhat paranoid. He lives in a park across the street from the welfare building. Jake doesn't have a phone, but he has a six-month bus pass.

After a few weeks Jake and I became good friends. We both consider each other attractive. He starts coming over the nights when my mom is working, and I let him shower and wash his clothes, and I feed him. In return he shares his crack and ice with me. Now I've started crack again. Such a pointless drug—you're only high for a few minutes, and then you need another hit. I so do not need three addictions, but I pick them up. My mom and my welfare don't pay for my drugs anymore. I start panhandling downtown. I have a sign that says, "Have a six-month-old baby at home with no food, no clothes." This sign works well, and I make from fifty to a hundred dollars in an hour of panhandling.

One late afternoon Jake and I are smoking crack at Mike's little closet room. An old man with no teeth keeps giving me rock after rock for free. After a few hours everyone gets up and leaves, even Jake. I try to go with him, but the old guy pulls me down and says, "Do you think I was just giving you my product for free? No, girl, you have to earn that crack." Then he takes down his shorts and pulls out a small uncircumcised penis and pushes my head down. At first I won't open my mouth, but he yanks on my hair and really tears it out. So I open my mouth and put his penis in it. He never gets hard, but he pushes my head up and down for twenty minutes. After he's done, he throws three rocks at me worth twenty apiece. He says, "You're such a whore I want to fuck you so bad." He kept putting his fingers in my vagina and taking them out and licking them. Suddenly Mike appears and saves me. I get up and leave right away. I feel so used and so worthless that I end up not caring anymore. I go to smoke crack every day at Mike's, and if some guy comes by and decides he wants to fuck me or for me to suck his cock, everyone leaves. I masturbate for men and let them suck on my nipples. Usually they are so jacked up or high on heroin that they can't get a hard-on. I smoke more crack and crystal meth to forget about it. It gets to be that three or more guys try to have sex with me in my time at Mike's using drugs. Mike gets sick of having to leave for a half hour at a time so I can turn a trick for drugs.

I get sick of this and stop going to Mike's cubbyhole. I start to go down by the river where the Samoans sell crack. Then one day I don't have the money to buy and want to get some on credit. Instead this big Samoan guy puts his hand up my skirt and pulls off my underwear and sniffs them. Then he takes me to a public bathroom and has sex with me. It's over in five minutes.

Every time I mess around with crack my life spirals out of control very, very fast. I can't stand men using me for sex anymore. Life was much easier when I was just using heroin.

Jake never looks down on me for my sexual acts with drug dealers. I only assume that he had to go through the same things being a broke drug addict brings. We never talk about it. Jake and I fool around every now and again in front of everyone at Mike's. He's the only one I want to touch me.

One afternoon I'm waiting for Jake to meet me at the bus stop less than a block from my apartment. We're going to buy some pain pills from one of Jake's dealers. We have our night all planned out. It's Jake's birthday, and his parents have gotten him a nice hotel room right on the beach on the twentieth floor. We are only going to use pain pills and smoke a little crack, eat out on the buffet, have prime rib and some wine, and go swimming at dusk.

As I'm waiting for Jake, a girl my age or so comes up to me and asks where she can find some smack. I look at her weird and ask why she would ask me when there are a hundred people around me. She says she can tell from my pinpoint pupils, and how gaunt I look. I ask her her name. She tells me Erin. She has an accent, either English or Australian. I ask her what she is doing in Hawaii. She tells me that she won this trip on a radio station. She's here with a group of people. I tell her I can help her out if she helps me out. I tell her who I'm waiting for and what we're about to buy. She thanks me over and over again and sits down with me, and we wait for Jake to show.

Jake shows up, and I introduce him to Erin. She wants to buy baby blues, 30 mg oxycodone instant release. She has two hundred dollars on her, I have eighty dollars, and Jake has twenty. Jake makes the call, and we walk a few blocks to the parking lot of some man's apartment. He is old and fat. He carries a backpack full of every kind of pain pill you could think of. I buy eight hydromorphone pills, Jake buys one cement mixer, 200 mg morphine, and Erin buys her baby blues. She also buys Jake two more cement mixers and me three more hydromorphone pills.

We start to walk back to our hotel room for the night, and Erin walks with us. We expected her to veer off on her own and go to get high. It turns out that we are staying at the same hotel. Jake and I check in and eat dinner. Then we got up to Erin's room and get high with her. We visit for a hour, and then Jake and I retreat to our room. We put on our swimsuits and hit the pool around 10:00 pm. After swimming we smoke some crack and take our pain pills and get really high. We end up falling asleep around 2:00 am. We aren't supposed to smoke in the room, but we do anyway and get cigarette burns in the carpet. It's all charged to his mom's card.

The next day I go home with my pills. I leave Jake with his pills and crack. I say to myself, *I'm never touching crack again.* This is on a Sunday. On Monday when the methadone clinic opens again I go there and have them raise my dose so I couldn't get high on heroin anymore. I still use Xanax every chance I got.

Jake and I stop hanging out so much when I stop smoking crack. My mom has stopped giving me money so easily. I am on a high-enough dose of methadone that I don't wake up thinking about getting high right away. I go a whole month without using heroin on top of my methadone. I'm ready to stop everything when I meet Garrett.

Garrett rides the same bus to the methadone clinic and home from the methadone clinic as I do. One day I sit by him. We hit it off as friends right away. He's a rockabilly type with short, slicked-back blonde hair and brown eyes. He's skinny and always wears black cuffed pants and a white T-shirt. By now I have been off junk long enough to get some sun and fill out a little bit.

One day I ask Garrett if he wants to go swimming, and after that we become best friends. Neither of likes each other sexually. He's hung up on his ex-girlfriend. Garrett lives in a van with his mom. My mom likes Garrett, and we have him over almost every night, feed him, wash him, and watch TV with him. Garrett always takes the floor, and I always sleep on the couch. After a while Garrett and I have talked about everything under the sun, so I ask him a question I will later regret. I ask him if he has a fetish. He says yes, but he can't tell me what it is because I won't understand. This gets me curious, and I hound him day in and day out about what his fetish is.

After about a month of me asking every day twice a day what his fetish is, we are walking home from the beach and pass a porn store. Garrett grabs my arm and pulls me into it. He takes me way to the back, and I think we are going into the gay porn area. He stops short of the gay porn and pulls out a video. On the cover is a beautiful blonde hunched over a man's chest, and her face is contorting like she is pushing. Then Garrett turns over the video to the back, and it shows women shitting on men's chests and men eating it on a plate with urine as wine.

I am shocked, but I don't want to make Garrett feel stupid or weird. So I say, "That's a strange fetish." I would have never guessed. We leave the porn store and walk back to the apartment. Garrett and I take separate showers. We take our swim suits out on the back porch to let them dry. Suddenly I feel uncomfortable with Garrett, and I start to talk too much. I ask him if he ever sneaked a peak at me pooping. He says no. I can tell I hurt his feelings.

After that we both have a few bucks, so we go to the Honolulu Tavern and sing karaoke for a few hours. We see Garrett's ex, Sara. Garrett wants to talk to her, but she doesn't want to talk to him. So we leave to go to the apartment and watch Conan O'Brian. When we get home, I take the couch and Garrett takes the floor. The end of Jay Leno is on. I am tired, and so I roll over and face the cushions of the couch. I am almost asleep when I feel someone behind me. I think it is just my imagination. Then I heard skin slapping together faster and faster. Suddenly I feel warm goo squirt onto my face and in my hair. I jump up only to see Garrett with his penis out masturbating over me. I yell at him, "What the fuck, man? You have to leave now."

Garrett is flustered and is running around trying to grab his stuff. He keeps saying, "Please don't be mad. You just looked so good tonight."

I get him out of the house and take another shower.

A few weeks later my mom is getting ready for work, and she wants to wear the diamond ring my dad bought for her. We can't find it anywhere. Then we remember the time my mom's gold necklace with the diamond in it was hanging out of Garrett's backpack. We just laughed it off as an accident. Now thinking back we realize that he was trying to steal it, so we call the police and put in a police report about a stolen ring worth three thousand dollars. The next day my mom is off, and we go to all the local pawn shops looking for it. We never find it. Garrett calls me a few times, and the one time I answer I ask if he stole the ring. He never admits to it; nor does he deny it. We never speak again.

Chapter 6

All this time in Hawaii my mom is either working or at the Honolulu Tavern hanging out with Scott and any guy who pays attention to her. She is sleeping around on my father, and with many different men. One night I walk in on a guy going down on my mom in the living room chair, and from then on I never walk in without knocking. Often nights I'll be sleeping in bed, and my mom will come home at bar-closing time and tell me to sleep on the couch so she can have sex with some guy.

Charlie still calls and leaves long messages on my voice mail about how much he loves me and how I broke his heart just like every other woman. He paid back the three hundred dollars we stole off that credit card we stole. If we ever run into each other in the mall I have to duck because he will come in to kiss me.

Jake and I say hi to each other in passing at the methadone clinic. I am clean and he isn't, so we really don't share anything any longer. About four months after Alex stole twenty bucks from me, I saw him and he gave me back fifteen dollars. He's so young to be strung out and homeless. I feel so bad for him. I never held his theft against him. If everyone was high in a room and I just got a couple of scraps, I would have stolen money too. I ask if he and Charlie ever speak, and he says no.

I never do tell my mom why I stopped hanging out with Garrett. She just assumes that it is because of the ring he stole.

When Christmastime rolls around I have no friends anymore. I spend all my time at the beach or across the road at the pool bar above the hotel next door.

By this time my dad has cleared out the house in Michigan, and luckily my aunts came up from Wisconsin and saved all the photos and relics. He gave most of the stuff away to Goodwill. He gave my two black dogs, Shawnee and Shasta, to a family friend and the two cats to two gay guys. He kept Eleanor for me.

Around this time my mom starts to talk about getting back with my dad. I call my dad and tell him this stuff, but he tells me that he isn't sure if he wants my mom back after what she did. He has been hurt too much. My mom stops going to bars and bringing guys home, and she cries to my dad on the phone that she wants him back. But he hangs up on her.

Suddenly one evening Mom and I are eating out at the Big City Diner when my dad calls me like he usually does every other day. But this time he asks to talk to my mom. They talk throughout dinner. She keeps saying, "I love you, Dean. I'm so sorry. We can work on this." When they finally got off the phone, I ask what happened. As we walk to the bus stop Mom tells me that Dad is flying down in three days and bringing us home to Wisconsin. I am elated but at the same time worried about going to jail in Wisconsin for running from my parole agent. I also need to get my methadone switched to Green Bay.

I know my parole agent thinks I'm in Hawaii, because I changed my address to Hawaii and he sent me a letter. I have a Hawaii driver's license. I also got a jaywalking ticket while living here. Even with the threat of jail looming over my head I am more happy that my parents are getting back together.

In one week we pack up all our stuff and put it in boxes to ship back to Green Bay, Wisconsin. My mom quits her job. Once my dad gets to Hawaii he doesn't want to stay in the apartment my mom was unfaithful in, so we get a hotel room. My mom and dad sleep in the same bed.

Before I know it I am waiting for the airport shuttle. We are leaving Hawaii, where I had good times and bad times. Once we get to the airport there isn't a second that getting caught isn't on my mind. The flight is long, but I just can't wait to see Eleanor. When we finally get home, my aunt is waiting for us with Eleanor. Eleanor acts like she don't know who I am. I start to cry, and my dad tell me that it will take a while. I think I had to leave her for too long.

We get to our new apartment building. It is a huge complex with hundreds of buildings in the complex. We have a swimming pool, a hot tub, a sauna, a pool table, table tennis, and a full kitchen in the building. No one has ever used this place, so it is like it is all mine. Our own apartment had a hot tub bathtub, a stand-up shower, two big rooms, a huge living room with a fire place, and a big kitchen.

That night I crawl into bed with Eleanor, who is now remembering me as far as I can tell, and sleep the sleep of the dead.

Epilogue

Back in Wisconsin, I worried day and night about the police. I never drove over the speed limit, and I always checked the lights on the jeep. While living in Green Bay we bought a laptop, and I found all my friends on MySpace. I started blogging myself. I started to read nonstop. I read the classics and the newer *New York Times* bestseller stuff.

One evening I decided to put pen to paper, and that's how this book came to be. It was as if the muse struck, and I wrote and wrote, and then it stopped. I was determined to finish it, so throughout the years I worked on it on and off.

My family and I were together with Eleanor, and that's all that mattered. We had been in Wisconsin for six months, and winter was fast approaching. My mom wanted to get a job in a warmer climate. The Hawaii army hospital called and offered her a job, so we as a family moved down there. I stayed off the heroin but relapsed on the Xanax.

I started to see a psychiatrist, and he diagnosed me as bipolar. He put me on mood stabilizers. I applied for SSI and got it. The only catch is that I had to do the jail time. We ended up living in Hawaii, this time for a year.

When we got back to Wisconsin, we moved to Oconto Falls, my hometown. I had gained a hundred pounds while in Hawaii with the mixture of methadone, Xanax, and my sweet tooth. I became a recluse, only seeing my family and walking my dog.

My parents got me a lawyer. He cost three grand, and I promised to pay my parents back when I started getting SSI checks. My lawyer set up a date when I was supposed to turn myself in, but as that date neared I got more and more depressed, and one night I slit my wrists almost on a lark. My mom found me in the morning. I ended up in the mental hospital for three weeks. From there the Brown County Police Department picked me up and drove me off to jail, where I ended up doing seventy-seven days. While in jail I cried often and missed my family more than I'd ever missed them. I got out just before Christmas, and it was the best Christmas I ever had.

Nowadays I'm totally off methadone. I used Suboxone to get off of it. I take all my medications every day. I get my SSI and worry that if too many of you read this I will get cut off—too many and not enough. I still live with my mom and dad and Eleanor. I'm on Weight Watchers, still trying to lose the weight I gained in Hawaii the last time.